Not With a Whimper

*Other Novels you
may enjoy by
Mitchell Rycus.*

*Rub up: Musings of a Navy Corpsman
(2007)*
The Noble Profession of Leaf Chasing (2010)
The Soil Is Dead (2012)
T (2013)
The Artist (2015)
Max's Fools (2015)
The Crooked Silk Road (2017)
*. . . and, Her Name Will be Called Hagit
(2018)*
*The Transmogrification of Esmeralda Bonnie
Watkins (2019)*
The Sad Saga of Angus MacTavish (2019)
Nostalgious (2020)
A Death in Detroit (2021)

CHAPTER ONE

The word first came out over the internet, then all the media followed: "The Surgeon General has recommended that the President authorize a national quarantine. No persons would be allowed to enter the country, with the exception of federally designated foreign officials, and no persons would be allowed to leave. We repeat . . ." and they repeated it. *What was going on?* The two young techies, Peggy Hammond, and Roger Wilson, wondered. They had already heard about some folks getting sick from an unknown cause, but a nation-wide quarantine? That seemed a bit of an overkill. They turned to TV news stations and the crawl on the bottom of the screen was identical to the announcement they heard on the internet. Regular programming was interrupted, and the usual talking heads were on instead under a red "Breaking News" banner.

"What's happening?" Peggy asked, as she sat down on the couch looking at the TV. "I just heard from mom that the country might be planning a lock down; have they said why?"

"No, I just turned it on myself after seeing it on the internet. It appears to be on all the major channels. This is NPR, let's listen to what they're saying." So the two of them sat there spell bound by the reporters who, one after the other, expressed shock and wonderment.

The news anchor at NPR was saying, "I was totally blind sided. I spoke with Washington no more than an hour ago and there was no mention of any national emergency. I specifically asked about the medical situation in California, and they told me it was under control. The CDC was aware of the outbreak and felt that it was manageable."

"Have they any idea as to why a shutdown might be needed? Did they say it was that contagious that such drastic actions were needed and. . ." the anchor woman started to say when her male counterpart cut her off.

"No, no . . . they've no idea how contagious or how deadly, or anything about it. I'm guessing they're just covering their asses in case it does turn out to be something really weird or . . ." he was saying when his co-anchor interrupted him.

"How do you know all that if you say they didn't tell you about a potential lockdown?" she asked her somewhat befuddled partner.

"I said, I'm guessing here." Then feeling chastened by his colleague he replied, "You're right, my opinion is not warranted, and I apologize to our audience for losing my cool."

Roger had to say something because this guy has always been very professional and never broadcasted his opinion as news. "Wow! This thing must be serious. I've never seen him, or her for that matter, so shook up over a story. Even wars, terrorist atrocities and major natural disasters have been coolly reported without a hint of emotion, but this thing . . . the idea of a shutdown has really moved this guy. Something really big is going on. I'm going over to CSPAN to see if anything is happening there."

Switching over to CSPAN they were surprised to see that normal coverage of the legislature was going on with poor attendance and no references yet to the Surgeon General's recommendation. "Are these assholes so blasé that they're ignoring the message, or are they so wrapped up in their own personal agendas that they could care less about the seriousness of a lockdown?" Peggy wanted to know.

"I think you hit it on the head; they're only concerned about getting re-elected and raising campaign money. Not one of these shitheads is talking about the potential for the biggest medical crisis since the Covid pandemic ten years ago. I'm switching to ABC; they do a job way better than this so-called public service channel."

On ABC their senior news caster, a soft-spoken Black woman was holding court with a panel of experts including a couple of senior members from the Department of Homeland Security (DHS). She had just asked them when the decision was made to recommend a lockdown of the US, and what knowledge drove that decision. The deputy director of Homeland Security answered her saying, "The decision on the part of the White House was in the making for a couple of days now, but when people started to die from—I guess—*the* illness in unexplained ways that clinched it. Also, the fact that so many had recently traveled abroad it convinced the president to at least consider authorizing the quarantine today," she said.

"The news never reported any illness being spread by foreign travelers, did it?" Peggy asked Roger.

"Not that I recall. Just some folks in LA were getting sick then suddenly dying, and they couldn't figure out why it was happening. They said that it just started a couple of weeks ago, but I don't remember them saying that enough were dying to require a lockdown. When the fuck did all this happen?" Roger asked, as an answer to Peggy's question.

"A couple of weeks ago according to the lady from DHS. But I never heard much about it either. Something screwy is going on here. I think the Covid pandemic put the fear of god into them so they're not wanting to fuck it up again like Donny did."

"You got that right. But, what's driving it? I think that there might be more than meets the eye here. I'm gonna do some internet searching to see if I can figure this one out. You want to get in on this?" Roger asked Peggy. She declined preferring to just watch TV to see if any new information was out there.

"I wonder what's happening in other countries; I'd like to know if any place else is considering lockdowns?" Hesitating a bit she asked Roger before he went into their office, "What do you want for dinner? It's getting late; do you want me to order a pizza?"

"Yeah, tha'd be fine. Put anchovies on my half," he said while leaving the room.

* * *

It was 2030, around ten years since the Covid-19 outbreak that originated in Kuala Lumpur, Malaysia, where it had first been discovered. At first it was thought that the Covid-Sars virus originated in China at their national virology institute, but it was found that the original virus jumped from a rat in Malaysia to a human in the city of Kuala Lumpur. The first incidences were mild and were treated as flu-like illnesses, not uncommon in the city's densely populated urban core, but as infected residents traveled to China the virus mutated to a more viral and lethal strain and populations around the world soon became infected.

"And the rest is history," Roger was telling Peggy later that evening over pizza.

"Too bad the Chinese got such a bad rap out of the deal. But that was primarily Donny's doing. All the hate and shit he launched. Why the fuck was it so important to figure out where it came from in the first place? Like the Chinese did it on purpose or something. Why couldn't they just accept that shit happens and just work on getting rid of it? I never did understand the world politics of the twenties," Peggy said.

"2029 was just last year," Roger reminded her. "It's still not clear what, if anything, has changed. I'm guessing that the current situation is also just a bunch of political shit to make us scared and want to keep the current administration around for a while."

"The politics of fear," she said, and after a pause she added, "I guess it worked so well for Israel and the Arabs that other so-called leaders decided that it would work here. After all Donny almost got away with it, and if he was just a little smarter he might have done it."

They sat there picking at the sesame coated pizza crust and drinking red soda pop while the evening faded. It was a lovely June evening, the current potential crisis notwithstanding. They had a busy workday, and the news of a possible quarantine was not a welcome bit of information.

They had only lived in their new place—Narragansett, Rhode Island—since January coming to town from New York where both were employed in the information science industry writing code and apps for systems unheard of only a few short years earlier. Being able to work at home in a small city was definitely appreciated and the fact that both were hired as a team made it even better.

There was not a lot of social activity in Narragansett Pier, but they were able to rent a magnificent New England style home on Perkins Avenue, just a short walk to the ocean. And the seafood was fantastic. The place was furnished in Early American décor—not their favorite style—but authentic Gansett so they put up with it.

It was an easy drive of around thirty miles, to Providence, the corporate headquarters of their home office, a high tech think tank, called Kolmogorov Industries. They would go in for occasional meetings and to touch base with their team leader. All in all, life was good for the two young techies originally from Michigan, that is up until the latest public health debacle of 2030.

* * *

Roger met Peggy in pre-school in 2000 when they were just four and two years old. Peggy's mom got the school to let Peggy join the three and four-year-old class because of her precociousness and language skills and she was potty trained. She was only two-and-a-half, but there was no doubting her ability and take-charge skills. Roger was smitten with the little red-haired girl from the time she walked into his class until forever after.

The two stayed close through high school, but they were separated in 2014 when Roger left for college but hooked up again ten years later in 2024 after Roger got his Ph.D. in computer science. Peggy had already got her master's in information science in 2022. The ten-year hiatus from close physical contact did not diminish their feelings toward each other, and both vowed to never leave the other alone again.

In 2025, they both ended up working in New York for the same engineering company and immediately decided to share an apartment and married life together as Roger and Peggy Wilson-Harmond. When the opportunity came for the two of them to join Kolmogorov in 2029, doing far more interesting work, a more flexible working environment and great salaries and benefits they took it. The had been living in Narragansett Pier for about a year when on June 25, 2030, they heard about the possibility of a quarantine.

* * *

The next day, Wednesday, their phone rang. "Who was that?" Peggy asked after Roger had answered the phone and shortly hung-up.

"Al; he wants both of us at the office tomorrow ASAP. I said we'd be there by nine."

"Did he say why? We were just there last week, and I thought we were all up to speed on our project. What could be so damn important that I have to get up early to drive to Providence?" Peggy wanted to know.

"Don't know, but he was emphatic. Sounded real important, like our jobs depended on it, so I said we'd be there. I'll wake you up early enough to make the drive in," Roger said, sounding a bit concerned about their latest development at work.

"Well, it damn well better be important for me to get up at seven in the morning," Peggy said, only mildly upset with the change in her routine.

"You know, Peg, I have a feeling that it might have something to do with that quarantine announcement, don't ask me why, but I just suspect that it does."

"Hmm . . . well that puts a whole new spin on it. Do you think it might be something like an Andromeda Strain thing?" Peggy asked, alluding to the mid twentieth century novel about a deadly alien pathogen that accidently comes to earth threatening to kill everyone.

"Don't know. Could be but seems highly unlikely. And if it was true, then why would a computer geek and information scientist be needed? We're more suited to work on algorithms that make products work better than dealing with epidemics. As I said, I've just got a feeling that's all."

With that proclamation the two science nerds went to bed, having a fitful night trying to sleep before the alarm went off early in the morning.

* * *

"Morning you two; hey and thanks for getting here so early really appreciate it," their team leader, Allen Phillip

Morris said as he walked into the small conference room where they were asked to wait. Al, as he was called by everyone, was around seven or eight years older than Roger and had a Ph.D. in molecular biology. "I'm sure that you've been wondering why the sudden meeting and more importantly why you two. Well, I'm going to tell you."

With that, Allen Morris laid out one of the weirdest scenarios either of them had ever heard before. If the Andromeda Strain saga was wild, what Allen told them was even wilder, and closer to home. But stranger still, was why this small team of two researchers were selected to do the work Allen was asking for. With all the senior intellectual power that Kolmogorov had at its disposal, picking two junior researchers to do such an important task seemed strange, yet made perfect sense when Allen explained the company's rationale.

"So, are you on board with this, or do I have to fire you?" Allen said, joking about firing them, but still emphasizing the importance of their participation.

"No, no . . . we're OK with it, aren't we Peg?" Roger said.

Peggy answered him, "I'm still not convinced that we're the best choice for the job, but I really don't know that many people in the company. Anyway, Al, if you think we're up to it, then I guess it's OK."

And with smiles and handshakes Roger and Peggy left but stopping before heading back to Narragansett to have lunch at a good restaurant in Providence. "So, what do you think?" Roger asked Peggy over coffee and dessert.

"I'm confused, that's what I think. I mean, what the fuck? He gave us no real logic as to why we were chosen, other than our technical skills, no other team members, no sense of urgency, even though he told us that people are dying, and the country may soon be under quarantine. But he seemed so blasé about it. Like it was just another assignment; '*Oh, by the way, do you think you could finish it by mid-July?*' he says. C'mon man, give us a break. You gotta show more enthusiasm, or anxiety than that!" Peggy remarked.

"Yeah, and here we are enjoying a great lunch while the country is in turmoil. I get it." Roger paused then said, "I'm thinking that Kolmogorov was asked to do an impossible job by somebody in DC, and it got passed down to us relative newbies. This way if we fail they can dump it on us, plus I'm damn sure that all over the world top notch research labs are setting up teams to do the same thing—find the cause and the cure, if it exists."

"So you do think that it is in other countries. Have any of them initiated a lockdown?" Peggy wanted to know.

"Not that I know of. Anyway, so, what do we know? He said a packet of stuff will be waiting for us by the time we get home. Why didn't he just give it to us during the meeting? His reason that he didn't want to go into detail over minutia just doesn't ring true. If it's not a biological thing then what the fuck is it?" Roger asked rhetorically.

Not waiting for Peggy to answer he continued his one-sided dialogue. "Do we feel comfortable looking for an inorganic solution to some kind of infestation that may or may not be organic in nature?" Roger mused, and again not waiting for an answer said, "Yeah, then why would they think that an information-based problem could in any way cause an epidemic that may be transmittable by people—" he started to say when Peggy finally cut in.

"And if we figured that one out then maybe we should be able to come up with some kind of an algorithm to stop it?" Peggy finished Roger's query to its logical end.

"Let's go home and look at all the 'minutia' that Al didn't want us to be bothered with at the meeting. Maybe we can figure out what in god's name is going on here."

* * *

When they arrived at their house a note was on their door instructing them to call a number for a package delivery. No other information as to who sent the package, or what was in it, just the number and the simple message. Believing that it must be from Allen, they called the number and identified themselves. In less than fifteen minutes a currier arrived, asked for identification, and then gave Peggy the package after she signed the delivery acceptance document.

"What's in it?" Roger asked as she came back into the house.

"Not sure. I'm just opening it—holy shit!"

"What is it?" Roger said, as he jumped up to see what Peggy was looking at.

"Will you look at these?" Peggy said, holding up what looked like X-Ray images of a human head.

"I thought that he said it was not an organic thing . . ." Roger started to say when Peggy pulled out the other documents from the package.

"Let me read this, OK? You look at the images and see if anything, other than medical information pops out at you."

Roger did as Peggy instructed, but for the life of him he could not see any indication that the images were anything more than traditional radiology scans. He had no medical training, so they were not especially useful. All he could do was make out the shape and structure of a skull, and some substance, he assumed was a brain, located in the cavity. There were around ten images all identified with a series of numbers located at the bottom left-hand side of the images. He also noticed that several of them were MRIs focused only on the brain, and he was even less familiar with CT or MRI scans.

"Well, this is interesting," Peggy said while sitting on the couch and reading the other materials. "It seems that the enclosed scans were taken from people who had recently died and believed to have been victims of an unknown pathogen. Medical doctors, physiologists and other related scientists could not identify the cause of death. Other than the diminished size of the brain no other abnormal physiological characteristics were noted."

"So, what does that mean? How are we going to figure out what killed them? If that's what we're expected to do. I mean, holy Christ, I have no way of even knowing where to start, do you?" Roger asked.

"Well, now that you mention it, I just might," Peggy said cryptically."

CHAPTER TWO

Kolmogorov Industries had prided itself on being a multi-disciplinary, cross-disciplined research organization using its employees, who were hired from a large variety of specialized backgrounds to solve problems usually attacked by a single discipline. Small teams of highly trained and seasoned researchers were given problems that historically could not be reduced to traditional STEM techniques.

By 2030, science and technology had dominated the methods of inquiry employed by industrial researchers for almost one hundred year. However, in recent years people trained mostly in the arts and social sciences began to creep into the corporate structure and were beginning to have their voices heard.

Administrators who were responsible for making their own businesses flourish monetarily noticed that enterprises who employed a multi-disciplinary approach to improve or enhance their product line seemed to be the ones outlasting their competition. Furthermore, think-tanks dedicated to cross-disciplinary problem solving were at the forefront of those organizations rapidly growing, and being hired by product and service-based companies to act as their research and development arms.

Roger and Peggy had been going over their package of materials for about three weeks using Peggy's approach of researching all ways that non-biologics could impact brain size. Much to their surprise there was very little information in the scientific literature describing or even recognizing an onset of abnormal brain reduction. Peggy felt certain that the autopsy data mentioning brain irregularities, even though it was only mentioned in some of the reports, was key to their subject's deaths. She felt that whatever it was that was causing brain reduction—once they knew that—they could then develop a prevention. Of course, Peggy's hypothesis assumed that it was the brain reducing mechanism that was killing the victims, even though none of the doctors who performed the postmortems said that brain reduction entered into their cause of death reasons.

***

"It's hot!" Roger said, "Even for late July. I know we're over a week past Al's deadline, but I say we give it a rest anyway and go to the beach. I know that Narragansett had warmed a lot since global warming picked up, but in ten or twenty years they say it should start returning to 1950 temperature levels again."

"Yeah, and if you believe that there's a bridge . . ."

"I know, I know; in Brooklyn you want to sell me," Roger answered Peggy's witticism about accepting outlandish offers. "Well, let's not wait years to enjoy a day at the beach, OK?"

People were still dying, but not as drastically as initially thought. There didn't seem to be a connection to overseas travel, so a quarantine was no longer considered by the feds, even though other countries, especially in Asia, were also still experiencing the strange malady. The UN was talking about setting up a special international investigation committee through The World Health Organization (WHO) to study the issue, but at present it was still just talk. There did not seem to be any known mechanism, nor any behavioral patterns associated with the deaths. However, very few children were affected, and no known cases had been discovered in infants. With these exceptions and unknown etiology the world looked on with fear and anxiety not felt since Covid-19 hit the world less than ten years earlier.

The major difference between the current health crisis and Covid was the lack of a contagion, so it was a less dramatic malady. However, the high mortality rate was indeed worrisome. It seemed that by the time someone was diagnosed with the syndrome it was too late to do anything and they died in a matter of days.

"I think we're out of options," Peggy was saying while they laid in the shade of a beach umbrella. The beach, although around a mile long seemed crowded for a weekday. But they still had enough privacy to talk about their problem. "I mean, we've beaten the small brain syndrome to death—excuse the metaphor—but you get what I mean."

"I think that the pathologists got 'Vanishing White Matter Disease,' mixed up with small brain syndrome. It doesn't matter since we still can't pinpoint either to the cause of death. Either way, late onset of either syndrome is exceedingly rare, and both are usually genetically based. None of our cases has had any genetic ties to brain issues, at least not according to the autopsy reports," Roger said.

"Even if it was genetic, all were too old, or too young, not to have someone notice something before," Peggy added.

"This is taking us too much into the field of biology anyway. Al said that we were chosen because we could see the non-biologic paths for such an epidemic, and here we are falling into the trap of traditional disease vectors. Not our area of expertise!"

"Yeah, but Kolmogorov prides itself on cross over research, so we're somehow supposed to know how to bridge the gap. I'm for thinking outside the box on this one. I don't think we understand enough pathology to talk about bio-pathogens so let's try the other causes," Peggy offered.

"Causes like what? Mechanical? Radiation? What areas are you suggesting we look into?" Roger asked.

"Well, I think bombs or other violent dismembering of bodies are obviously out of the question," she said in a sardonic way, "but I think mechanical mechanisms might be OK. Remember the sound wave weapons used in Cuba, something like that might be worth investigating. Or the Russian killings of their dissidents using radioactive polonium. I mean, there are thousands of ways that these people were made victims that doesn't need a biologic origin."

"Thousands! You got that right. So, where do we start? I think we need a more disciplined approach, and not look at a simple bubble sort. And what dataset do we use to sort on anyway?" Roger asked Peggy, the information scientist.

"Don't know just yet, but I'll get on it and get back to you, OK?" She responded, again in a casual manner.

* * *

Both had been exhausted trying to satisfy their boss' request, and now that their report was overdue, and they had little or nothing to show for it, they were beginning to get on each other's nerves a little. They seemed to be blaming each other for not having made any progress, so their interactions were getting a bit chippy. But making the decision to stick strictly to non-biological causes for the mysterious deaths gave them focus and forced them to go down roads that other researchers may have missed.

"How far out do we want to take this. I mean, are extraterrestrials out of the question?" Peggy asked the next day while they worked at home on a very rainy Friday.

"Hmm . . . not certain if we're equipped to go there, but like what were you thinking?"

"Not sure yet, but if we want to look at things that others might not be looking at I just thought that ET might be an avenue to pursue. You know, sort of like lateral thinking. If this is something that has never been seen on Earth before then maybe it's from outer space. That kind of thinking."

"You mean like something brought in by meteor dust—"

"No, that brings us back to biologics. Maybe something to do with messing up our lives just to see how smart we really are. You know, like testing our capabilities to really solve existential problems with absolutely no known etiology. Not enough to make us extinct yet, but potentially able to cause very serious damage if we don't solve it," Peggy said in a very thoughtful way.

"And who do you think is doing this? Testing us? Or are you worried as to who, or what, may be causing the problem more than curing the ailment?" Roger asked.

"I honestly don't know. I guess it's the old chicken and egg problem; do we focus on the cause or the consequence? Simply knowing the cause may not rid us of the problem, and somehow by mitigating the consequences it doesn't address the issue of why it's here in the first place and could it somehow come back even deadlier."

They were both quiet for a while thinking about what they had just put together and trying to figure out a plan of action for them to take under the set of parameters they just uncovered, when their phone rang.

"It's Al," Roger said, instantly recognizing the incoming call number on his cell.

"Answer it. I've been expecting him to call. What are you going to tell him?" Peggy asked.

"Hi Al," Roger said cheerfully, although anxious about what he would say to him.

"Yeah, I know we're past due on that last one, but It's far more complex than we first thought." Allen must have asked Roger something as he paused and then said, "Huh? Our approach? Well we've decided to concentrate on non-biologics since we feel that people with more knowhow than us are already doing that." After a pause while Allen responded, Roger was smiling and gave Peggy a thumbs-up sign while nodding yes. "Yes, yes, nothing else is off the table. OK, then, we promise to have a preliminary report in a month or so. Thanks for your vote of confidence. Yeah, see you in the office next month. Bye,"

"So what did he say? I take it we're still on the problem," Peggy said.

"Yeah, he's glad that we came to the conclusion to leave the medical or biological stuff for others and concentrate on other areas of inquiry. But he's still anxious to see something so he wants us in the office next month to report on our findings. He sounded a bit harried and must be under some kind of pressure. I'm guessing that his medical research team is also stalled, so I guess we have our work cut out for us," Roger reported.

"I say we put together an action plan and then get on it. Three weeks of research and a week to put the report together; does that sound OK" Peggy offered, as Roger nodded yes and then the two without further ado started to write on their laptops knowing exactly what the other was doing. Peggy was putting together an outline while Roger was listing specific areas of research they'd pursue. They knew each other's work habits very well.

* * *

It was a classic New England day in late August when the two went into Providence to make their report. Fresh breezes were running off of Narragansett bay with fair-weather clouds scampering across a bright blue sky. Providence was busy as people were preparing for school to start in a week or so, and the long labor day weekend was already getting some of them to make an early start on the holiday.

"Good to see you two, got a lot of folks anxious to hear your report," Allen told them as they came into his office. "We've got the large conference room scheduled; expecting around twenty-five people," he continued as he led them over to the conference room.

The room was set up for any kind of report format, either PowerPoint, slide, or lecture-discussion presentations were available. Peggy and Roger knew that they'd be ready for them, so they prepared a PowerPoint with around forty slides, and handouts for ten people. "Looks like we'll need more handouts," Peggy commented as she took a look at the size of their audience. A young man took a copy of their handouts and ran out to make another twenty copies to have enough for today and several left over for any future demand.

"You all know of our Hammond-Wilson team and their investigation as to the causes and impacts of the Diminished Encephalon Fatality Syndrome. Some of you have been working on the biological aspects of the problem, while Peggy and Roger have focused their research on non-biologics and today we've asked them to give us an update on their findings. So, without further ado, Peggy, Roger, the show is yours," Allen said by way of introduction.

"Thanks, Al. Roger and I don't know many of you but over the last year or so we've had the opportunity to work with some of you on several very interesting projects, but this one trumps them all," Peggy said, and watched as heads shook with knowing expressions on their faces.

Peggy started the presentation with a brief overview of the causes and symptoms of other noncommunicable diseases (NCD), and how Diminished Encephalon Fatality, or DEF as it was now apparently being called, in no way resembled any class of the other ailments. Also, the etiology of most NCDs are well established and there are only a handful, such as poisons, which are fatal in such a short period after detection. But even so, the cause of death, other than the heart stops beating, is the only causal relation associated with DEF and death. No lesions, tumors or other pathological abnormalities are noted on death certificates in any postmortem exam.

Roger took over with the PowerPoint show demonstrating how various forms of death may occur, other than by disease transmitters. But the diminished brain size was a stickler. There were no known, at least to him, diminishing brain conditions that seemed to appear without any prior causal relationships such as heredity or old age-related factors. But even so, why such a condition would cause death so rapidly is totally inexplicable. Even in dementia patients and Alzheimer cases small brain size, or white brain reduction, does not seem to play into such a rapid death prognosis.

Most of their audience knew these facts and were getting restless, wondering if the team of Peggy Hammond and Roger Wilson had anything new to offer, or if they were just repeating what most of them already knew, when Roger hit them with a bolt of lightning that woke them all up.

* * *

"Well, I must admit that your critical Factor Analysis got their attention," Allen said after the presentation. "Even I was beginning to wonder if you two had anything new to offer, or what, but you did a great job in getting your point across."

"Thanks for the vote of support, Al. So, what now? Do we get a team to work with us, or what?" Peggy wanted to know.

"C'mon, Peggy, you know that that's not up to me. I'll take your report to management and hopefully get their approval to authorize the team of investigators you've outlined in your work proposal. Assuming they agree, where do you want to continue your project? Do you want to come here, or open a place in Narragansett?"

"If it's all the same to you, I think a small workstation for say ten people in Gansett would work best for us. Do you think you could swing that?" Roger asked.

"OK, I'll see what I can do. I have faith in you guys, so I'll do my best to get all the approvals. It would be no mean task for Kolmogorov's people to solve this new global threat, so I would expect that it's a done deal. But don't go to the bank on this just yet, OK?"

Peggy and Roger left in the early afternoon, on a still glorious day in Rhode Island, after being taken to lunch by Al to celebrate their latest discovery, or more realistically, their path to an earth-shaking discovery. Now all they needed was the breakthrough to operationalize their theory, and that's where the real problem lay.

* * *

"How did you like the groans when I told them about our hypothesis?" Roger asked Peggy when they got home.

"Well, I expected nothing less when you said it so casually; 'climate change.' So much ecological phenomena have been attributed to global warming I would think that veteran researchers, like our colleagues, have grown desensitized to the issue," Peggy answered.

"Yeah, but our examples of bees and coral polyps did the trick. It got them thinking that if a whole species can be negatively affected by climate then why not us?" Roger said.

"Yeah, why not us? Good question, but we still need to come up with the mechanism that causes the issue and trace it back to climate related events. I hope Al gets approval for a research team to work with us. I told him that I'd like an ethnologist on it, but he said that he hasn't gotten that far yet."

"So you still think that cultural behavior is a significant factor. You said that before, but you never told me why. So, why do you think that culture plays a role? Climate change could care less about our behavior once we fucked up the world's eco system so badly," Roger said.

"Because the way the syndrome seems to attack people from all over the world. I think once we find the similar factors that either skips over some people or selects others to become stricken, then we'll need to closely examine their behavior and that's what ethnologists do; differentiate cultural behavior," Peggy answered.

"But group behavior is not necessarily the same as individual behavior, so why ethnologists?"

"I don't know, it just seems to me the right approach, that's all. We've examined a lot of individual behavior and its yielded nothing so far. So why not consider group dynamics?" Peggy said, not too convincingly.

"Well, whatever, as long as we have a good statistician on our team I think we can do it with big data sets at our disposal," Roger said. "Anyway, I'm certain that a medical type will also be on the team because, like it or not, dying from unknown causes *IS* a biological disorder."

* * *

And so Kolmogorov Industries put together a team of five researchers and an office manager in a small office complex in Narragansett to tackle the issue of DEF with a mandate to either solve the problem or close shop in one year. They would have until October 1, 2031, to come up with a working theory on the cause and treatment of DEF or expect to be reassigned. Kolmogorov was committing several million dollars to the effort but senior management felt that it was its obligation to society and so they budgeted the project into their corporate research agenda.

It also helped that a team member, Andrew 'Andy' Roscoe Kataev, was the grandson of Kolmogorov's founder. It seemed that Andy's, great grandfather, Nicolai Kataev, was the famous Russian Mathematician, Andrey Kolmogorov's, father. Kataev, was not married to Kolmogorov's mother and was not involved in his upbringing. He disappeared in 1919, but his family knew who Kataev was when he wound up in New York at the height of WWI and served the government as a Russian expert. Kataev's son from a subsequent marriage, built Kolmogorov Industries naming it after his famous half-brother, Andrey Kolmogorov. Kolmogorov Industries now employed the youthful Andrew Kataev as one of its young research mathematicians.

Although Roger and Peggy were the titular group leaders of the DEF project everyone knew that it was Andy Kataev who, as the heir apparent to Kolmogorov Industries, was the real boss. However, Andy did not throw his weight around and was an honest team member willing to do what he was asked rather than impose his own agenda on the others. Also, he was a world class statistician and looked forward to being in on the resolution of DEF syndrome.

The other group members making up the team were Laticia Betty Langerforth, the Ethnologist and Ga Eun Marcel, the Medical Doctor. A racially, and gender diverse group of five people with different values and research capabilities.

"So you think that it could be caused by stress," Roger asked Dr. Ga Eun (pronounced jee ay yen).

"Climate induced stress is a possibility, but requires a considerable amount of research to validate," she answered.

It was their first official staff meeting in their Narragansett location away from the Kolmogorov campus in Providence. The company, realizing that their work would draw a lot of attention preferred that the DEF facility be off site, so they accepted Roger's suggestion that it be located in Narragansett.

They found an office complex in South Kingston, just a couple of miles from their house. Their complex had a small suite consisting of an open office area, a conference room, two separate offices adjoining the open area, but one desk in the open area was dedicated to Rozamarie Antion, the office manager.

No other spaces were individually assigned but the five researchers worked at a desk, a table or on the outside patio, or wherever they chose to. Computers were on site and individual laptops connected to Kolmogorov's secured network were given to each team member. It was a very laid-back place with no set hours of operation and people could come and go as they pleased with each having 24/7 access to the site.

All would be working together to rid the world of just one more climate related crisis while the rest of the world worked on trying to handle the original global problem of trying to cool the planet back down. Both issues were existential threats, but it appeared that DEF was the only one threatening human populations. Several people thought that that wasn't as important as saving the whole planet, while others felt that human extinction was the only issue worth addressing.

But politics would not be part of Peggie and Roger's problem, or at least that was what they had hoped for. However, as it always does, the political reality of the situation grew overwhelming huge and threatened to capsize Kolmogorov's whole agenda.

CHAPTER THREE

The election of 2032, even though it was still two years off, was beginning to loom large on the horizon as the former VP was finishing off her second term as president. The 'in' party had not anointed a favorite candidate and it looked like the field was wide open to a bunch of lackluster wannabes claiming to be the country's best choice. All the candidates claimed that if elected they would solve the DEF crisis, but none of them had contacted Kolmogorov's DEF team.

Roger's Factor Analysis had been widely disseminated since his presentation in August, just last month, demonstrating that areas with more significant climate change disruptions, like fires, floods, droughts, and higher than normal temperatures showed significant correlation to DEF cases. Also, being a victim of DEF correlated with the factor of their family being more likely to have moved into the area they lived in for at least three generations.

At the DEF team's office, the only time everyone was expected to be in the office was Monday, 11 AM, for brunch and to report on progress. Roz—Rozamaire's nickname— would have a large buffet of bagels, sweet rolls, coffee, tea, and juices, and all the trimmings laid out. Enough food in case the meeting would last over the two hours scheduled. She also recorded the whole meeting and was free to join in on the discussion even though her academic training was limited to a two-year business curriculum from a community college.

Roz had previously been employed for over twenty years at a few high-tech places and learned more than most by just listening. She loved working for Kolmogorov's DEF Group with its small staff of brilliant researchers and when she found out that they would be involved in finding a cure for DEF she was excited beyond words.

The meeting started out with Peggy asking Andy the statistician, "What do you think Andy? Factor Analysis work for you?"

"Factor Analysis or Cluster Analysis; both would give us ideas as to where we should spend our time. Unfortunately, as you all know correlation is not causation, so even if we have a smoking gun we still need to know what made it go off," the future owner of the company said.

"Oh, bad analogy," Laticia said, making Andy blush a little. Seeing that she embarrassed her co-worker she quickly backed off saying, "But I get your point and that's all that really matters," she said much less judgmentally. "I like the fact that it seems grounded in space, and that it seems to have effected subjects whose family now seems to hang around in one climate zone. As an Ethnologist I find that most noteworthy and would love to work on that element of the problem, unless somebody else wants it," she said.

Not wanting to appear to be sucking up to their future boss, nobody else commented on Andy's remark, but Ga Eun commented, "Yes, correlation is not causation and Andy's right; we have to look at what could have caused those individuals who were subjects of some severe climate influences to just suddenly die. I would like to look at that element."

"Well, I guess that leaves everything else up to the rest of us," Roger said in a half joking manner.

The meeting continued well into the afternoon as the team was well fed on bagels and sweet rolls and seemed to enjoy just getting to know each other. They all liked what they were seeing from their co-workers and some very lively exchanges took place when around three in the afternoon Roz said, "I think if we're going to go on much longer you guys may want to consider me ordering up dinner for this evening."

"Why don't you all come to our house for spaghetti? I've already made enough sauce for four or five dinners so it's all right there?" Roger suggested. Nobody said that they couldn't make it, so in a couple of hours they all packed up their laptops, got on their bikes or cars and drove over to Roger and Peggy's.

On the way over Andy stopped to pick up a nice Italian red wine and Ga Eun found a bakery with fresh Italian bread. So, the dinner party was set for any time after five at Peggy and Roger's house on Perkins Avenue. It was another magnificent early fall day in September and the sun was moving into the west sky promising a glorious early fall sunset. The DEF Group was still high on each other and anxious to start really working on the global issue while drinking wine and eating spaghetti. They all felt that the world was in synch with them and they would accomplish remarkable things.

* * *

After dinner, sitting in the large front room, drinking chianti, and eating spumoni they relaxed when Roz asked, "Do you all mind if I tell you a few of my thoughts about today's meeting?" she asked.

"No, I would very much like to hear your take on our plan. You've been around think tanks for a long time and I'm curious to know what you think of our little group," Roger said.

"Well, first off, I think that all of you are brilliant, and I'm thrilled to be a part of the group. When I first read about Kolmogorov on their webpage I got excited to be offered the job. What excited me was to see that the company conducted action research on complex issues in multi-disciplinary ways that the researchers would cross over into other areas outside of their expertise. And that they'd be working in small groups like yours." Andy was smiling taking the compliment personally.

Roz continued. "Now I've worked for R and D places of all styles and in my experience I found that the most successful were those that used a cross disciplinary approach. That's why today I was surprised to see you folks asking to work on tasks primarily in your own realms of proficiency." Roz paused before going on, and then saying, "I had a boss in one of the places I worked at who told me that all his researchers thought that everyone else's problems were more interesting than their own. So he would assign them work to do in those areas for which they had no previous expertise or even basic qualifications. That company was the most successful place I ever worked in."

"And where are they now?" Laticia asked.

"Gone. Taken over by corporate raiders who drained them of their valuable assets, and then bankrupted them. Greed drove them first into mediocrity, then non-competitiveness, and finally incompetence finished them off."

"Who were they?" Peggy asked.

"RI Solutions, one of the premier think tanks in Rhode Island. That is until the shareholders wanted more money on their investment and brought in the raiders," Roz said.

"Yes, that's a story we heard often in the 1900s and early 2000s and even now. Hey, but that's the way capitalism is supposed to work; isn't it?" Andy asked.

"No! That's not the way caring and responsible leadership is supposed to act. I've seen both types of management styles—responsible and greedy, and greedy always loses out in the end. Oh sure, some corporate top-level people come out of their greedy companies super wealthy, but the vast majority of the employees come out with zilch. And society loses corporate leaders and innovators in the process as well."

"So, how do we look as a potentially successful research organization?" Roger asked Roz.

"Oh, you guys look great, but if I might . . ." Roz hesitated like she was asking for permission to talk.

"Sure, go for it," Roger told her.

"Well, like I said you all need to expand your horizons. For instance, I would have Andy and Laticia looking on the medical factors involved, and Ga Eun and Roger doing the climate-based side of the question. Then Peggy would be free to examine the methodological applications necessary to tie the whole thing together, with some help from Andy of course, and I can still manage the office without all of you running around like chickens with your heads cut off," she finished on a humorous note to lighten the day's events for her younger colleagues.

Roger was quiet for a while before responding to Roz's suggestions. "Sounds like a worthwhile model. But, it's getting late, we've covered a lot of ground today. How about we all sleep on it and maybe we can meet tomorrow afternoon to say whether or not we like Roz's assignments, or how else we might want to work together for the next year." There was a silent agreement from the group before wishing each other all good night.

* * *

"I thought our first staff meeting went really well, and wasn't Roz a surprise? She's something else; I'm glad she's working for us, aren't you?" Peggy asked Roger before getting in bed.

"She makes lots of sense. After all, we hired her to manage the office, so I guess she's taken the job to heart; managing," Roger said with a smile.

The next afternoon everyone was in the office, and after minimal discussion as to what everyone's role should be, Roz's model for working was adopted with the caveat that at any time someone wanted to change their role they could. But they had to let Roz know what aspect of the problem they would be working on and who else they would be collaborating with.

And so the hard part of doing research with or without other people to bounce their ideas off of began. The computers and laptops were abuzz with activity, as well as their cell phones. But it was the landlines into the office that proved the most disconcerting to Roger.

It seemed by then everyone in the world was aware of the group and wanted to know what they had to say about their approach to solve the DEF problem. However, a strict protocol was established and all external enquiries were directed to the corporate public affairs office. Roz was a pro at being able to put people in touch with corporate and not bother everyone with questions for which no answers would be available.

The staff was strongly urged to stay off social media for the duration, but under no circumstances were they allowed to discuss their work outside the confines of their workspaces. Only Roger or Peggy was allowed to talk with outsiders about their efforts, but even then it would be limited as to how much they would divulge and what each researcher was working on. It was a bit confining for such free-wheeling scientists to get used to, but they all understood the gravity of the issue and the need to prevent a media circus fomenting around them.

A sleepy tourist town like Narragansett Pier was an ideal place to have such an operation like the DEF Group. The few townspeople who were aware of them minded their own business and also protected the small DEF research group's privacy.

Kolmogorov claimed that they had received funding for the DEF project from a private investor who wanted to remain anonymous. But the investor's organization was also told that they could not interfere or contact the DEF Group directly and needed to get all their information from the company's VP of product development. If their benefactors were not pleased with the arrangement they could cancel their obligation, but they would not receive any compensation for monies already spent. At times, this arrangement was hard to keep, but Kolmogorov kept its word protecting their DEF Group from outside pressures.

* * *

When word somehow did leak out that the Kolmogorov DEF Group was focused on climate change as the key element being considered as the causal link to the syndrome the far-right wing of the government was determined to stop the project claiming that Kolmogorov was totally off base. They accused Kolmogorov of having a leftist agenda (after all, the company was named after a Russian) and needed to be stopped from *spreading more fear and distrust into an already overburdened and highly regulated corporate world.*

What was especially sad was that the American born doctor, Ga Eun, was being accused as a Chinese operative with the task of blaming America's manufacturing industry for causing the global illness. It would have been laughable, if it was not for the death threats she began to receive. The fact that she was of Korean ancestry wasn't even noted by her detractors. Nor was the fact that for most of her life she was called Jean because people didn't take the trouble to learn the correct pronunciation for her name.

Even her fellow lab rats at Kolmogorov were simply told to call her Gee so as not to screw up her name. But Ga Eun hung in there with support from the crew. But then Andy Kataev began to get smeared as a Russian sycophant and as the future CEO of Kolmogorov Industries could not be trusted as a loyal American. He too was lumped together with Ga Eun as a combo who were out to destroy America. Laticia, as a Black female was branded as a Black Lives Matter proclaimer. She would work with her foreign comrades to bad mouth America as a country out to destroy the white men who dominated the world's ruling class. Roger and Peggy were simply dupes of these foreign agents. Only Roz was not implicated in the group's contrived treachery, which bothered her for not being included with her fellow co-conspirators.

"You bet I'm pissed! Don't they think I'm smart enough, or good enough to fuck up the world? Well, they got trouble now because they've stirred up Rozamarie Antion's Italian blood," Roz said as she was reading an on-line far right blog about the DEF Group.

"Don't even think of dignifying them with a response," Ga Eun said as she saw Roz getting angrier and angrier reading the document.

"But they are mentioning everyone in the group by name and leaving me out. I'm a full member of this group and I deserve to be as fully vilified as my more noteworthy colleagues. They're doing it just because I'm an old lady and age-sexism is something I won't tolerate," she said, half tongue in cheek.

In a couple of seconds after hearing the phone ring, she picked up and in her distinct New England Italian dialect said, "DEF Group, Roz speaking. How can I help you?" Ga Eun watched as her face reddened and she could see that Roz was about to explode, but she angrily hung up the phone and sat there very upset.

"Who was it?" Ga Eun wanted to know.

"Just some asshole. We need to get an unlisted number for the office, or else have all our calls come in through corporate. Do you think our boss would do that?"

"Don't let them get to you. We can handle them, after all they are really just a small group of troublemakers . . ." Ga Eun started to say.

"Yeah, but they have support from a major political party in my country and that shit has to cease! I'm upset, and rightfully so when outrageous claims and downright lies are made, and good people are being attacked for trying to save the world from horrible consequences due to decades of neglect and greed. In some sense I wonder if this world deserves saving," Roz said shaking her head. "I'm glad that both my parents didn't live to see this day, and that I never had kids that would have to live through this kind of a world." Pausing a bit she continued in a more subdued manner. "Don't get me wrong, I'm a good Catholic and believe in the mercy of God, but at this time in history I think God's fuckin with us just too damn much; forgive my French," she said.

"Amen," Ga Eun said, and the two sat there in their own thoughts wondering what other indignities they would suffer in the days to come. They didn't suspect then that the ultimate indignity was still to come.

CHAPTER FOUR

The world was truly bifurcated along ideological lines; vaccinators and antivaxxers, science based rational reasoning and anti-science irrational reasoning, and even professional sports was dragged in with Cleveland finally renaming their baseball team from the Indians to the Guardians and then being accused of erasing history. And on it went, almost fifty-fifty since the advent of the Trump administration almost fifteen years earlier. But it seems to be happening everywhere in the world and not just the United States. Left versus right wherever you look, and it didn't seem to have an end in sight. That is until DEF was introduced.

"I have to admit that the only good thing that might be coming out of all this is that the world seems to agree it needs solving, and along with some other countries they're looking to us for answers," Allen Morris was telling the DEF Group over a Zoom meeting. "I know you find that hard to believe with all the chatter you're getting on the social, but trust me worldwide polls are showing that finally there seems to be some universal agreement . . ."

"That's because they're scared shitless," Andy interrupted. "Believe me, the rate of increase in mortality rates are beginning to have their effects, and nothing scares someone more than dying from an unknown cause."

"What do you think about all this Andy? You're a statistician; is it truly unknown causes or just bad diagnostics?" Allen asked him.

"I've checked and rechecked the data and I'm telling you something really new is out there. Historically, in western countries where I have access to this info, SADS, or Sudden Adult Death Syndrome with or without an abnormal brain size historically has been extremely low amounting to around point one percent. It's now clocking in at close to point two, or a one hundred percent increase. That should scare anybody. Now that's including all the known causes of SADS that have been accounted for, so this is something we need to answer quickly, and if it is, as Roger and Peggy believe climate related, well I don't know what we can do about it."

"Then it's all over unless we really can turn the abundance of global CO_2 around. We're working on that, but will it be in time? We have to get this right or the world as we know it is gone," Laticia interjected.

"The world is depending on these kids and others like them in other countries to solve it. I'm betting on them to get it right," Roz said.

And with little else to report Allen Morris encouraged them to continue working. He too was worried about Andy's data of such a stunning increase in SADS, most likely due to DEF, and could only hope that the small, but elite group of researchers was up to the task. Maybe he should have insisted that a more experienced staff from Kolmogorov's list of employees should have been selected. But rather than second guess their choices he stuck with Roger and Peggy's selections. Though, he was pleased that Roz was there to keep them on point, if anybody could inspire a young group of scientists she could.

* * *

On Halloween day, Thursday, October 31, there was an afternoon party at the DEF Group office to commemorate a month (or so) of being in business and generally smooth sailing. Though no major breakthroughs were on the horizon, work was progressing with each member getting comfortable in their roles. Roz had bought wine and cheeses for the party and bought some goodies at the local bakery, so the group was getting a little high while Roz passed out silly masks for everyone to wear in order to get into the holiday spirit.

Around six in the evening after a couple hours of revelry Peggy said, "I suppose we should get home soon just in case the neighborhood kids are out trick-or-treating."

"Yeah, they TPed my place last year, so I'm staying up tonight to catch them," Laticia said.

"And what will you do if you do catch them?" Ga Eun asked.

"Well, hopefully with this werewolf mask I've got on, I'll scare the shit out of them," she said.

Everyone laughed, knowing that Laticia was a caring person who would not hurt kids on a night devoted to pranks. But Andy was a different person. "If I caught the little bastards messing my place up I'd make them clean it up or spend the night in jail; their choice," he said, not smiling.

"Lighten up, Andy. It's Halloween, for Pete's sake. Didn't you pull pranks when you were a kid?" Peggy asked in a good-natured way.

"No. Our family didn't observe Halloween, nor any other devoted to pagan rites. And, in my neighborhood the kids didn't roam around in gangs begging for candy. I never understood why they did that. Didn't their parents give them sweets?" Andy asked.

Everyone was a bit taken in by Andy's deprived childhood, but nobody said anything at first, until Roz said,

"That's sad, Andy. You know until the pandemic of years ago I would say that most of America looked forward to this . . . to this *pagan* rite. Halloween, like Thanksgiving, at least outwardly are non-religious affairs. Yeah, I know that some folks made both of those great days religious events of sorts. But anyway, I would hope that if you ever do have kids you won't deprive them of this simple pleasure. I do assume that your family did celebrate Thanksgiving, didn't they?"

"Yes, yes, of course we did, and Christmas and July fourth, we are Americans, even though some would have you think otherwise. No, it was just Halloween that my folks didn't like I guess. I had parties in my elementary school, but no costumes or candy, all too frivolous. But to answer your question, yes, if I was to have children and my wife wanted it we would let the kids party. I'm not a Grinch," Andy said, this time smiling.

"Good to hear," Laticia said, "I knew that beneath that cool reserved exterior beat a heart of a wild man."

"Well, I wouldn't go that far," Andy countered.

Soon the banter ended, and everyone went home. Roz stayed behind to clean up and wouldn't let anyone stay to help her. "You kids go to your families and enjoy the rest of the evening. I suppose that I'll see some of you tomorrow, and if not then I'll catch you all at Monday's meeting. Go, go, I got this.' Roz said moving everyone out the door.

"Would you two, hang for a bit," Roz asked Roger and Peggy as they were about to leave. "

Agreeing to stay they sat down while Roz told them her concerns. "I think that Andy is having problems and may need some talking to. I think that he's overly sensitive to his role, and it might be affecting his mental health. Do you know if his parents are involved with his work life?"

"Gosh, we don't know. His dad *is* the CEO, but we've never personally met him. We've just assumed that Andy's serving some kind of an internship before moving up to management. Do you think we should let Al know?" Peggy answered.

"Might not be a bad idea, but you guys need to keep an eye on him too. I've seen this happen to other overly involved research scientists and the end is not always pretty. I'm hoping that Kolmogorov has a mental profile on record for him so that they can step in if it gets really serious."

* * *

The hybrid work environment of home and office worked well for the DEF Group and having flexible work hours, was very productive. But the Monday staff meetings were mandatory and on occasion they were joined in a Zoom meeting with Allen, or one other member of his team in Providence. One such meeting happened on Monday, November 4, just a day before the federal mid-term elections, and Allen had requested that their meeting be Zoomed.

"It looks like the Dems are gonna loose seats in Congress," Allen was telling the DEF Group, "so, I suspect that our role in DEF may be diminished—no pun intended—but I just thought you all needed to be informed." Allen was making light of the fact that the 'D' in DEF stood for diminished.

"Does that mean that we'll soon be out of work?" Peggy asked.

"No, no, you'll all be assigned new work, that is most of you, but we still intend to fund your effort with internal funds. I wouldn't worry, just letting you know how things stand."

"You said most of us will be reassigned, who will be let go?" Roz asked.

"No, nobody will be laid off. I meant that some of you will still be working on the DEF project. I don't know who just yet, but all of you will still be Kolmogorov employees, OK? Is that clearer?"

"Yeah, sad but clear. We're just getting into it so it's too bad we have to get hit with this shit," Andy said.

Roger was quiet during Allen's announcement, but he was noticeably shaken. "Fuckin' politics. Don't those assholes realize how important our work is?" Roger said to his team after Allen Morris left the Zoom meeting.

"Why don't we wait to see the election results before we write off our efforts?" Ga Eun said. "I don't know where Al got his election forecast from, but everything I read said that it's too close to call either way."

"Even if the Dems lose the house, they still will have the Senate, so I don't think that our program is doomed. And, by the way, when was our program federally funded? I thought we had private funding from an unknown benefactor," Laticia said.

"I think that private benefactor might have been a rumor. But you know, we've never had any government watchdog agency show up to look at our books, or ask us about our progress, and that seems kind of odd," Peggy said.

"Peggy's right. Maybe I can use my connections to find out what's going on here," Andy said implying that his status as the heir apparent to Kolmogorov Industries would give him access to information that nobody else on the DEF team had.

"Go for it," Roger said. "What good is having power if you don't use it, right?"

* * *

By Wednesday afternoon all the results were in, and the Republicans had taken the house by a razor thin two seat margin. The Dems, as expected still controlled the Senate by their thin margin of five seats, so filibusters could still control legislative efforts, but seemed to be less a hurdle as the world became increasingly nervous over DEF.

DEF was an allegedly 100 percent fatal ailment that showed no signs of slowing down and was continuing to grow and cause anxiety all over the world. The fact that it could be caused by climate change was not strongly agreed upon by various factions in the international scientific community since it was so long in being recognized. Particularly after the effects of global warming had already been well documented, DEF was a late bloomer. The world wasn't ready to accept another climate induced catastrophe even though there was compelling evidence that a number of global issues (e.g., storms and floods, severe wildfires, species nearing extinction) were already attributable to climate disruptions. But humans being impacted so directly, well that was not acceptable to some people, especially to the religious conservative movement which was certain that god would not allow that to happen.

The Christian right formed the base of the Republican Party, and their support was thought to be necessary if they were to stay in power. That extra clout seemed odd since they were only a minority segment of the party. So, it was not surprising that their spokespeople poo pooed the idea of climate change as being a cause of DEF and wanted to see all research and development efforts to cure the ailment directed to medical and spiritual (i.e., religious) efforts. They were proposing massive amounts of funding to faith-based enterprises who focused on prayer and good-Christian living habits to solve the crisis. And even their medical efforts were strongly aimed at supporting Christian based medical institutions.

"Have we heard from Al yet as to how the election is going to affect us?" Peggy asked Roger late Wednesday afternoon.

"No, nothing out of corporate has come our way. I told Roz to let me know immediately if Al was on the horn. I'm gonna assume that we're all right, and we should just keep working like nothing's gonna change. I'll check with Andy to see what he found out when, or if, he comes into the office. In the meantime let's stick to business as usual. I'm meeting with Ga Eun later to winnow our approach to the climate issue."

"Speaking of Andy, I wonder how he and Laticia are doing on their task? Peggy asked Roger.

"Haven't heard from either of them. Maybe we can ask everyone for an update on Monday," Roger said.

* * *

By the end of November the political climate had settled down, but uncertainty was in the air about the future status of the DEF Group. Andy was pretty much a loner and liked to work by himself. He was not thrilled to be asked to work with Laticia—someone he thought was practicing pseudo-science— to partner on medicine, a topic he was not the least bit interested in or knowledgeable about. But as the future CEO he felt obligated to do what his father asked him to do, and spend five years in the pits, before moving up to management. This was his second year at the company and his most important assignment to date. He was determined to be a good soldier and do the best he could for his company and his family.

"I'm more comfortable working with abstract theorems and models that involve math, then I am with medical data," Andy was telling Laticia, working at his apartment in Narragansett. They agreed to work there since it was nicer than Laticia's place and had an excellent view of the ocean.

"I know what you mean. I'm more comfortable in the quantitative social sciences than in the medical arts too, but I guess we should give it our best shot," she told him.

Andy was pleased what he heard from Laticia about her attitude toward scientific inquiry. As they began to work closer together it seemed that the two fell into their work as if it was meant to be. Soon they had developed a medical model that could be investigated rigorously as to the cause and effects of DEF and were on their way to finding some answers.

In the meantime, Roger and Ga Eun were working on the climate element when Ga Eun noted that in her experience stress due to weather changes caused a number of, mostly non-fatal, conditions in humans. "Like what?" Roger asked.

"Mostly emotional symptoms like general ennui, depression, you know, we've all had those down in the dumps symptoms caused by bad weather stretches," she answered.

"You know that in engineering long term stress on metals can have the same impact as one instantaneous large shock. Has there ever been any physiological factors associated with DEF conditions?" he asked.

"If you mean other than the diminished brain size, I don't think so. Then again, I'm not certain if any other specific biological studies had been associated with weather related disorders."

"Then let's do that—look at the climate conditions and emotional stress histories of the victims. That just might lead to the link we've been looking for."

"I think on Monday we need another update to bring everyone up to speed on what we're guessing at here. Also, we need to let Peggy and Roz know what data sets they need to get reduced for us," Ga Eun said, excited that they now seem to have a pathway to explore for their task.

* * *

Roz was not educated in computer science, at least not formerly. However, at Enspirate, a think tank she worked at in the sixties, she was asked to learn APL—an early programing language—to aid the researchers who were carrying out their calculations on slide rules and adding machines. If they could get their calculations done quicker and more efficiently on their new IBM 1620, then that would go a long way to give them a leg up on their competition.

Roz, later took a crash course in FORTRAN II, IBM's newest programing language, and became proficient enough to head up the company's small computer support lab. Even the companies that she worked at after leaving Enspirate still employed her programming skills to manage many of their office operations. It was not a far reach that she would team up with Peggy to help negotiate the huge data sets that were required for them to access. Of course, she did this along with all her other duties as office manager.

By Christmas of 2030, with ten months left on their one-year mandate to find the answer to DEF, the group was on its way to meeting its goal. They also felt comfortable enough in their approach and finding success that even if they were terminated before October 2031, they would have come close enough to claim victory. But life has never been that predictable, and future events would make their sure win a little less certain than they felt at the office party on Monday, December 23.

"I propose a toast to all of us," Roger started to say raising a glass of champagne.

"Hear, hear!" the others shouted raising their glasses.

"Al, and corporate, have been silent on our status lately, and even Andy here has been taken out of loop, but in spite of our roadblocks we prevailed. We got this thing, and we will save the world from annihilation!" Roger shouted.

"Hear, hear!!" they again shouted back, with smiles on their faces and even though most thought that Roger's claim was a bit grandiose they relished the possibility of imminent success.

After they all drank from their glasses Roz stood up and said, "As the senior member of this team, well at least age wise, I just want to say how much I love you guys. No, really, I mean it. You are the smartest, most dedicated team of researchers I've ever had the privilege of working with in my many years of work in R and D." Looking firmly at the group she said to them, "No ego! No backbiting! No scheming! Just dedication and that's what you all bring to the table. Thank you, so would somebody pour me another glass," she said as she held out her empty for a refill.

"Let's hear it for Roz, the glue that holds all of us together," Laticia yelled, and they all loudly cheered.

A little tipsy, Laticia needed help sitting down, but Andy was right there to help her, and Roz immediately noticed their obvious dynamic. She didn't say anything, but she knew the signs of an office romance and filed it away for future reference. *Maybe Laticia could be just what Andy needs to keep him on track*, she thought and hopefully Roger and Peggy wouldn't have to get involved on Andy's behalf.

After making certain Laticia was safely seated by him, Andy without standing, and a little nervously began to talk. "I just want to say that I endorse Roz's observations whole heartedly. I know some of you think I'm just a corporate spy, but as Roger pointed out in his toast that nothing could be further from the truth. Yeah, some day I might be up there with the other suits, but right now I'm just another working stiff like you all are. And nothing would make me, my father, and my grandfather prouder than knowing that I took part in one of the company's major contributions to humanity. So, here's to you my colleagues, and I'd also like to believe my friends, for treating me as an equal."

When he finished, Laticia leaned over and gently kissed him with tears in her eyes. After seeing Laticia's response Roz felt that her thoughts about Andy's mental state no longer being an issue now, were well reasoned.

After that, the talk all changed to holiday plans and being home for them. DEF issues were not mentioned and after having a catered dinner brought in, compliments of corporate (maybe Andy misspoke about him thinking he was just another worker) the team, well-oiled on champagne and booze, loudly and joyously savored their holiday treat.

CHAPTER FIVE

Progress for the DEF Group had slowed down considerably by the spring of 2031. After an enthusiastic start with much promise for the team's goals none of the three smaller teams had made much progress. Allen Morris was noticeably short tempered on their April 21, Zoom meeting. "You told me all that a few weeks ago, and even then you didn't have anything new to report. Look, are you making progress or are you just treading water?" he asked noticeably impatient. "I told you that things might get rough after the midterms, and they are. The board is pressuring me to either show some real progress—not the pulp fiction you're serving up here, Roger—or turn you lose. So, what's it going to be?"

"Gee, Al, I didn't know that we were under such a strict schedule to show you breakthrough results just midway through our project . . ." Roger said, a little short tempered himself.

"Yes, you did. I let you all know how things stood in November, so don't tell me you weren't aware of any deadline. Look, let's cut to the chase. You need to show me something I can hang my hat on by June, or I won't be able to keep you afloat. Now before you all get hung up over that, I'm promising that you all will still be employed by Kolmogorov. But the DEF program will be over. A number of countries are working on it, and we'll just have to let them take the lead.

Alright, this meeting is over," and with that last pronouncement Allen signed off.

"Holy shit! Was that some kind of a bum's rush, or was it something else?" Laticia asked to no one in particular.

"I guess he did tell us in November that things might change, but to all of a sudden jump on us like that, wow! Well, at least this time he said all of us, not just some of us, would still be employed. I still, can't say I'm not disappointed," Roz said in a gloomy voice.

"But we seem to be so close. What an asshole to jump on us like that," Andy said.

"He's just doing his job," Laticia said, trying to calm Andy down. "I'm sure he gets his orders from management, and they probably told him to put the pressure on us. I'm guessing he wasn't too happy to have to tell us that, so let's not be too harsh on the guy."

"Laticia's right. We haven't come up with anything worth crowing about. In fact we're not too far past page one, so we shouldn't blame Al," Ga Eun said.

"Look you guys, we got till June, so let's just forget Al's motives for now and take stock in what we do have," Peggy said. "Where are we right now, and do we have any chance at all of meeting Al's latest deadline?" she asked the team.

"I think that we're about to validate the climate cause hypothesis with a high probability of rejecting everything else," Roger said.

"Our medical model is also rejecting pathogens with great regularity, so what's Al want from us?" Laticia wanted to know.

"If all of that's true, then what's the cure? And if we don't know that, then what have we really accomplished, if anything? How can we treat climate change like a *pathogen* to stop all the deaths? More importantly, how can we save the fuckin' human race from annihilation?" Andy asked, rhetorically.

"Jesus Christ, Andy, I don't think that's in our pay grade. If we can just prove, to within a reasonable accuracy our major premise about climate change as the most probable cause of DEF, then I should think that we've really carried out our mission," Roger said.

"From an academic viewpoint you're right Roger, but for all practical purposes if we can't come up with a valid treatment we've failed," Andy countered.

"We've been so wrapped up in finding a non-medical cause we haven't even looked at cures. Do we even have time to start looking at cures now that we have only a month more's effort left? Are any subjects surviving, and if so, what were their treatments?" Ga Eun asked.

"If I may," Roz broke in, "Why don't me and Peggy get all the data on Ga Eun's question, while the rest of you go on a balls out effort to answer her. I think the cause you came up with is close enough established, so that leaves us a month to save the world."

"Roz is right," Roger said. "Let's just break it up to diagnosis, treatment, mortality, and survival. So, who wants to do what?" Roger asked.

"I'll be glad to do treatment," Ga Eun said.

"I'll take diagnostics," Andy volunteered.

"I guess I can look at survival, that's something ethnologists know a little about," Laticia acknowledged.

"Then I'm stuck with mortality rates, assuming it's really not 100 percent," Roger said.

And so the team, reinvigorated with their new goals went on their various new paths to tackle their mandate.

* * *

Over the long Memorial Day holiday Roger and Peggy got word that Allen's ultimatum was not carved in stone, but he certainly hoped they had something for him by Monday, June 16, or he would have them re-assigned on July 1.

"Well, it gives us a couple more weeks, and at least that's something," Roger was saying on Tuesday, May 27. They were having their Monday meeting a day later to accommodate the holiday. "Are we gonna make it guys? Are we close enough to answering our questions, or are we on the chopping block?"

"Nobody's getting chopped," Peggy quickly retorted.

"Yeah, but you all know what I mean. We've put our lives on hold for this project, so stopping it now would be very hard for us, I'd think. Anyway, what the fuck! So, who's got anything new to report?" Roger said.

"All the data that Peggy and Roz came up with on treatment from around the world pretty much showed the same thing. And I want to compliment you two on finding that data, getting it all translated into English and getting it to me. That was a heroic effort. Anyway, the various treatments were astounding, even though most treatment facilities had only a few days to observe their patients before they died," Ga Eun began her presentation.

Almost as soon as she started Andy cut in with, "Yeah, and most of the diagnoses weren't made until after postmortems. Even then, most death certificates listed cause of death as *unknown*. If it wasn't for the smaller than expected brain size, DEF wouldn't even be on the documents. But in later data, as the number of deaths increased DEF became more frequently noted as a probable cause, and if it wasn't for early MRI's and lack of response to known treatments, as few as there were, we would have no data. Ga Eun can attest to that, right?" Andy said looking a Ga Eun.

"Were any treated in ways that showed any promise of surviving?" Roger asked. "Because I found that in some places the mortality rate was not total. Did you see that too Laticia?"

"Yes, I did! And that's what gives us hope for a cure. It's not definitive, but some kinks in DEF's armor were noted based on Ga Eun's analysis. Why don't you tell them?" Laticia said to Ga Eun, following up on Andy's request.

Ga Eun told them about how in a Hmong village in southern China a few cases of apparent DEF were diagnosed that hadn't killed their hosts. If it wasn't for the modern hospital system in the region they never would have been able to discover the syndrome, but what was really astounding was that modern medicine did not have any role in their treatment. All known Hmong survivors of diagnosed DEF were treated by 8,000-year-old east Asian folk medicine.

Ga Eun continued with her premise. "Well, I'm not sure the treatment was the cure. It's based on ancient Chinese folk myths involving incantations, herbs, and other unproven treatments. As a doctor, I've heard about these so-called homeopathic remedies, but much beyond a simple headache none have proven beneficial in treating serious conditions. I would see no reason to think that now all of a sudden they would work on DEF."

"Yes, that may be true, but if this is the only place where we actually have survivors, and the only treatment they received were these ancient ones, then I would say that's convincing evidence to seriously check it out," Andy answered.

"Actually, the Hmong village was not the only place to have seen survivors of DEF," Ga Eun said. "I noticed other small pockets of survivors in a few other places around the world where we have data: an Inuit community in Canada, a small village in Honduras, a village in Siberia, and an isolated community inside Nigeria. But no known urban regions had such pockets. At least, none were noted."

"So people can survive! Well, that's encouraging," Roger said.

It may have been good news, but unfortunately since no known treatments or use of any modern technology was noted, and since in most cases even the primitive treatment afforded the Hmong survivors was not listed in any detail, it was not much help. With the exception of finding out that DEF's mortality rate was not 100 percent, nothing of use about the Hmong incident was found useful.

"Andy, can you do a very complex factor analysis on those places where we have at least some data on DEF survival to see if they have anything at all in common that might explain their unique survival profile?" Peggy asked.

"Yeah, of course I can, I just need to know what factors I'm looking at."

"I'll help you with that," Laticia said, as Andy's face brightened knowing that she'd be working closely with him again.

"I'm assuming you can do that in a week, right? The rest of us will keep on looking for pockets of survival, and if we notice any parameters that Andy needs to consider in his analysis we'll get it to him STAT!" With that last announcement Roger ended the meeting.

* * *

The next Monday everyone showed up on time anxiously waiting to hear Andy's and Laticia's report. Nobody was interested in knowing how SPSS, the statistical analysis package that Andy used, works, just the results of their analysis was all they wanted to know. After Laticia laid out the factors she thought they needed to investigate like, social adhesiveness, climate change, population density, cultural identity, and other mostly social and hard to measure variables, Andy focused in on the medical and demographic ones. He chose age, sex, health, marital status, and other personal data that might be available to enter in the model.

They both agreed on treatment methods and diagnostic results as well. But, with so many variables to start out they were afraid that the results would be watered down to the point where no meaningful results could be identified. And because the total number of survivors they had data on was less than two hundred they kept the level of analysis at the individual level rather than the entire community. This led to a significant amount of diversity within all the data, but it paid off when the final results were revealed. As the model cranked out correlation indices associated with each of the factors for all the survivors in all the communities a pattern emerged.

"Holy shit!" Roger said. Can it really be just that simple? I mean, we've been saying this all along, but now we have a statistical model to validate our original premise."

"Well, yes, climate change seems to be the strongest indicator, explaining the most variance in statistical terms, but not as obvious as we had hoped for," Laticia said. "It seems that all the communities where DEF mortality was less than one hundred percent, were places that had experienced a significant amount of climate change.

"But the people who survived were from families who had migrated there thousands of years earlier, in other words, Aboriginal Peoples." Andy said.

"What do we know about where they migrated from?" Roger asked.

"We did a thorough ancestry check, and where available, genetic research on each of them and have gone over the tons of data they provided. But further analyses did show that the vast majority originally migrated from areas with relatively stable climates. Places that had not suffered the extreme summers and winters like the places they lived in when they became afflicted."

Ga Eun, getting into the spirit of the discussion said, "I wonder if somehow their systems had been genetically affected by their transition into a less stable place. Maybe they somehow were genetically selected to survive the effects of climate change and not be killed by it?"

"So, are we saying that somehow—don't ask me how—those of us whose ancestors came from the same environmentally stable regions on earth are the ones most likely to survive?" Peggy asked.

"It isn't certain. But it seems having centuries of genetic roots living in a relatively non-climate affected area, and then migrating your family to a climate affected area, well your chances of survival increased. But why you got sick in the first place is still an open question. We still have a host of other variables that show some modest, but not insignificant correlations, to look at more fully," Laticia said.

"You mean variables not related to climate change?" Roger asked.

"Well, yes and no. If climate change is the most likely variable determining who lives or dies, then what other underlying variables—specifically genetic variations—are in play here. I mean, why do some of the victims who have similar family histories die. But most important, how can we know in enough time to find the ones that are going to die and then save them? That's the trillion-dollar question," Andy said.

After more talk about Andy's and Laticia's discovery they decided to continue along the path of climate change as the primary reason behind DEF. Ga Eun said that she'd be glad to research environmental stress as a causal factor in death, and possibly even in microcephalia.

Andy and Laticia would continue to work on their model of climate induced factors in DEF. Roger said he would help Ga Eun in any way he could, while Peggy and Roz kept at data gathering about anything on DEF that might be the least bit of interest for Andy and Laticia's analyses. They had around six weeks left to get the job done.

* * *

Two weeks later, on June 16, they decided to have what might be their final meeting in a restaurant near the water. It was during a late spring heat spell, and they all needed a break from the intensity of their work, so a late afternoon dinner meeting was called for.

Roz arranged for them to meet at the Coast Guard House, a restaurant where they could sit outside and smell the cooler easterlies blowing down from the north Atlantic. Even though it was a major tourist area in mid-June, it was still nice to smell the salt air and hear the calming ocean waves while listening to the cries of the terns, and just enjoying their colleague's camaraderie. Roz arranged for two tables to be put together on the eastern most side of the terrace, and they had enough privacy to talk freely and still enjoy the food and view.

"Two weeks, ladies and gents, just two more weeks and then we're toast," Roger said with a half-smile of acceptance to the inevitable.

"I think we've shown enough progress to be given more time," Laticia said, "what do you think, Andy?"

"Don't know. I agree, hon, but it's not up to me. In spite of what you all may think about my position I really have no more influence than any of you all right now. I wish I did, but I don't . . ."

"Hey, man, stop putting pressure on yourself. We know the deal, so don't you go thinking that you'll be letting us down if we get axed next month," Roger said, trying to support his colleague.

Peggy jumped in; "Look you people, even if the project is ended we will all be working on something that's probably just as important, so let's give it a rest. We did our best and found out a lot of stuff that those who will follow through with will find invaluable. I'm certain that the world's scientific community will resolve the issue . . ."

"But if they don't we are toast, and I mean everyone in the world not just the six of us," Andy finished on a very down note.

They were all quiet for a minute when Ga Eun said, Peggy's right. I think it's just too big a problem for just the six of us. And why haven't we heard from other scientists around the world. Only the media with their spokespeople who claim to have talked with *'experts'* who say results are just around the corner. What do they know that we don't?"

"Well, one thing is certain, we got the world not to shut everything down like they did with the Covid pandemic. At least they were smart enough to realize that DEF is not transmitted from living creature to living creature by any biological vector. I don't know, I just think that maybe our approach might be wrong . . ." Roger started to say when he was angrily interrupted by Andy.

"Well, for fuck's sake, then just how should we have done it? If you have another approach, or for that matter, if any of us have another approach that we thought would be more effective then why didn't we speak up? We did it the right way; maybe we weren't the right team."

The talk stopped while the team digested Andy's anger. After about five minutes of silence, with the exception of the surf hitting the rocks and the cry of the seabirds punctuating Andy's tirade, Roz spoke up.

"Well, if everybody's done beating us over the head I think that we need to continue with this meeting on a more positive note. We've done more this last month than in all the previous months we've been together, so I expect that our *NEXT* half-month—notice I didn't say our *LAST* half-month—will be our most productive one yet. Doesn't anybody have some good news?" Pausing for a minute she continued. "Well, if not then I guess what Peggy and I discovered mucking with the data might just interest you. Do you want to tell them or can I?" Roz said looking to Peggy for approval.

Peggy looked a bit confused, so she just said, "No, no—you go ahead and tell them."

"Our latest discovery, or I should say, possible lead to a discovery was that we think we found precursors here in the United States for potential DEF survivors. Now, we haven't exactly found any yet, but based on the cases from other countries we think that we've seen some evidence of who might survive. More important, who has already survived. If that is true than that's something we can all hang our hats on, don't you think?"

Peggy looked at Roz as if to say, 'when did we find that out?'

"Now, it's all in the very early preliminary stage, and of course Andy and Laticia will have to verify the statistics, but if it is true . . ."

"When can you get us the data?" Andy asked.

"I don't know, tomorrow sometime?" Roz said looking at Peggy to answer.

Peggy, still a bit befuddled by Roz's statement said, "Uh, I guess tomorrow, or certainly by mid-week; we still need to do some data cleaning, but I guess by Wednesday. Roz and I will be getting together right after this meeting to discuss it further," Peggy added looking a bit troubled at what Roz had postulated. When nobody said anything else, Peggy noted, "You realize that Roz's comments are very preliminary of course, and still need work to verify our results," as a way of preparing them for any possible let down.

As everyone got ready to leave Peggy pulled Roz aside and quietly told her to meet her at her house STAT!

* * *

"What kind of shit was that!" Peggy said as the two of them met in her house just a few blocks away from the restaurant. "Where did that come from? I never said that, and you never told me anything at all about finding those kind of results, so what the fuck were you doing?" Peggy was noticeably angry, and Roz knew it.

"It's called a pep talk, or whatever. We needed something to get their spirits up. Roger and Andy's doom and gloom attitude was about to completely destroy any hope for a new sense of purpose, so I just did what I had to do. C'mon, Peg, you know we needed something to keep us going, so I improvised. But, and I repeat, BUT there is a chance I'm right. We've been wallowing in the data for a long time now, and I just have a sense that something has been missing from our results; a thread, a motif, sometime to tie it all together. I know there has to be one. If we just organize the data in the right way, Andy and Laticia should find it. It won't take me long to create a couple of relational databases for Andy to do his magic. Look, I promise to have them done by Wednesday, so let me try, OK?"

Peggy stared at her older, and apparently wiser colleague, and then got up and hugged her warmly. "God love ya," she said.

* * *

On Tuesday everyone showed up at the office to watch Roz and Peggy put together the data sets and offer any insights or help that they felt important enough for them to consider. Andy was the most active literally looking over the two women's shoulders at their computer screen to see if he could spot something they might have missed.

"Looking good, ladies," Andy said, and then he said, "I can see my analysis unfolding just watching you two work, but make certain that Laticia goes over your variables, OK?"

"We *ladies* will be glad to do that, Andy. Why don't you go make yourself useful and get off our backs for a while, we've got this," Peggy said, taking issue with Andy referring to them as ladies.

"Huh? Oh, sorry, if I'm getting a little antsy, but Roz's announcement at yesterday's meeting has really got me pumped. If we can predict who, who won't die from DEF, well then that's something the world will really latch on to," Andy said.

"Yes, it is important, but I wouldn't bet on the world being very appreciative. Only if what we find out leads to a cure or prevention will people be happy. And if it isn't our group who figures that part of the puzzle out, well then we'll just be another footnote in the field of scientific inquiry, but no Nobel Prize," Roz said.

Andy looked a little saddened by Roz's remarks, and spotting this she said, "Hey, but who said that we were in this for the glory. Either way, we, or some other group comes up with a solution based on your analysis, Andy, you'll have scored it big in ours and the company's eyes."

If one looked closely one could see Peggy surreptitiously winking at Roz who smiled knowingly that some people's egos needed a little massaging from time to time.

CHAPTER SIX

The precursors that Roz was referring too were a little fuzzier then Andy had thought they'd be, like diet, spirituality, and other personal mental and physical health parameters. Unfortunately, lots of individuals in their data did not have all the information they would have needed to come up with a definitive answer as to why, or how, they survived DEF.

But even more complex was that the list of sudden adult deaths from the national database was sorely lacking in a lot of personal data on the victims. Andy was using this database to see if the precursor data from the international files fit into the victims here, and if so, then he'd compare that information to national mortality data. It was a slow and tedious process, which offered limited hope of finding any tangible results that could lead to finding survivors of DEF in the states—but it paid off!

On Monday, June 23, Andy and Laticia presented their preliminary findings to the group. It was not the silver bullet that everyone was hoping for, but it was enough to keep them engaged, and that was exactly what Roz had hoped for.

"The correlation coefficients are very small, but not totally insignificant," Andy was saying when Laticia added her thoughts.

"What Andy said is true, but that's from his quantitative viewpoint. My qualitative side says that we have more to cheer about than we've had in a long time. When I aggregated the variables I saw that certain parameters seem to stand out more than the individual data might show. And after reading interviews with the afflicted and hearing their stories I see a thread that shouldn't be ignored—family support. Yeah, yeah, I'm hearing your skepticism loud and clear, but as an ethnologist I'm familiar with these indicators and I'm certain that we've found one here."

"Sounds a bit murky to me," Ga Eun said, "but I do know that in certain clinical situations the support of one's family can make a difference as to the outcome of some serious diagnoses. But there are so many factors that go into family involvement, like clinical care, financial stability, tight knitted members, and very stable families versus unstable ones. I mean, how are you going to put all that together? And even if you do, what level of reliability do you expect your prognoses to have?"

Andy offered in a very surprisingly succinct way. "Well, we didn't say that we found the cure. All we said is that we seem to have found one indicator of survival, and even then only in some of those countries where we discovered survivors. It's still not clear that 'family involvement' has anything to do with survival here in the states, but that's because we don't know who survived. The SADS data base only lists deaths, not survivors, and anecdotal near-death cases where patients ultimately survived are legion. Folks, I'm telling you we have a very difficult problem here, so if just one thing, like family care, seems to work then let's employ Occam's razor and use it for all its worth."

"Andy's right. Like I said, mucking with the data Peggy and I thought that a thread was there, and he and Laticia might just have found it. So let's go for it gang," Roz said.

* * *

Allen gave them a two-week extension since they claimed that they'd have some real results to show him by mid-July. The team worked as one unit doing whatever each could do to firm up their hypothesis that climate change caused, and family care cured DEF. The initial findings of diminished brain size in postmortems seemed to wash under the bridge as an outlier event and was not believed relevant to any causal relation. The final task of tying cause and cure together for a solution was needed and that's what the team focused in on.

On Monday, July 7, after the long July Fourth weekend the team met for their final time as a unit to receive their marching orders of what each would do over the next week to prepare for their meeting with Allen the following Monday. Peggy and Roz had the important job of taking everyone else's input and putting it all together as one cohesive PowerPoint presentation.

Allen had scheduled them to meet with him and his staff in Providence, on Monday, July 14 at nine in the morning. Roger and Peggy would be doing most of the talking, but other team members could jump in whenever they felt it was necessary.

On Sunday, July 13, Roger, and Peggy showed up at their office to rehearse their presentation. The other members were asked to just rest up that day and be prepared for anything on Monday.

"That's it! It's done, we're through. I think we've done one hell of a job on this, and I think that if we can convince them to operationalize our suggestions we have a good chance of beating this beast," Roger said.

"Yeah but convincing them is going to be hard since we have no real clinical data that our cure works. I don't know, Rog, I think this is it. In fact to tell you the truth I think they'll laugh at us. Only the fact that survivors original roots were from previously stable climates before moving into unstable ones when they were hit with DEF seems to be provable. All the rest is conjecture at best," Peggy said.

"So, are you saying we walk in with our proverbial tails between our legs and plead for mercy from the court of Al and his staff? What then? They give us another month? Fuck it! We go with what we have and hope that the rest of the world jumps in where we left off and gets the job done," Roger answered.

They were quiet as they went one last time through the presentation, looking at their slides with Andy's data splashed periodically throughout to give it a look of quantitative scientific credibility. But no matter how hard they tried to convince themselves that their boss and his advisors would listen to them, they couldn't help but feel defeated.

* * *

"Good to see all of you here, and I'm looking forward . . . no, make that the *world is looking forward* to your presentation. With the increase of DEF rates occurring all over the world I don't have to tell you how important your work is. So, without further ado tell us what you've discovered," Allen Morris said by way of introducing them, and putting them under even more pressure to produce.

Roger started by first introducing Peggy, his co-leader, and then the rest of the team in alphabetical order. He didn't say what their background education was so that their work would be judged on its own merits and not on the expertise of any individual.

Allen and his staff politely listened to the entire presentation only interrupting occasionally to get further clarification on a point or two. After the half-hour PowerPoint show Roger asked for comments, but more importantly, he asked for continuing support to carry the project into a final stage of having a fully operational plan to implement their findings.

Roger was met with deafening silence from Allen as a way of what Roger perceived to be total rejection. But Josephine Allison Ginsburg, Allen's senior advisor, and a very distant relative of the former Supreme Court Justice, Ruth Bader Ginsburg's husband, spoke up.

"I love it! I love it! Finally, some serious scientists believing in qualitative analyses enough to stake their professional reputations on it. Now, don't get me wrong, I'm not totally convinced that I think everything you've done is strictly kosher and deserves immediate attention, but I do think you've made a case for your hypothesis that calls for further investigation." Then smiling directly at Laticia, Josephine Ginsburg said, "I'm guessing that it was you that did that, the qual stuff, well you go girl," she finished.

Ginsburg, who was called Allie by everyone, had a Harvard law degree and an MS in Mathematics. Her boss, Allen Morris, had such respect for her that he seldom disagreed with her decisions, so a deep sigh of relief ran through the team after Allie's most favorable proclamation.

Laticia was visibly embarrassed being called out like that and said, "Thanks, Allie, but it was all of us who did the research and I'm proud to be associated with this team."

"Well, I for one didn't love it as much as my chief of staff here, but I do agree that it at least deserves further study. Roger, if we were to grant you time and money who else would you want on your team?"

"To be perfectly honest with you Al, we haven't taken it much further than what we showed you today. Can we have another week or so to come up with an action plan that would include a budget and timetable?" Roger asked.

"Sure. Do that. Just let me know when your plan is solidified, and we'll decide what course the company takes. In the meantime, you all just keep on doing what you're doing because like I said, the world waits. If we're done here, then we'll hear from you soon."

After the presentation Roger took the whole team out to an excellent restaurant in Providence for a late lunch before driving the team back to Narragansett. It was an extremely hot mid-July day, and all of the team was so upbeat that they didn't even notice the heat, nor did they comment on the presentation.

All was right with the world and Laticia and Andy announced their engagement at the restaurant to loud cheers and champagne toasts. They said that they planned to announce today only if they got a reprieve but would wait until some future day if the team was axed. How fortunate for all that things turned out as well as it did.

Later that evening, back in Narragansett, Roger and Peggy were relaxing and getting ready for bed while they watched the news on their bedroom TV when they heard the reporter say, "Good news tonight; Kolmogorov Industries announces breakthrough in DEF disease and hopes for an early cure. More on this later."

"Oh shit!" Peggy was saying when the phone rang. The caller ID showed it was from Roz.

"Have you seen it? The news?" Roz asked even before Peggy could say hello. "I guess we should be prepared for a shit storm tomorrow, but if you like I'll handle it like I did in the past," she said.

"We appreciate that, so yes, please take care of it," Peggy said. After finishing with her conversation with Roz, Peggy looked at Roger and said, "I guess it goes with the territory. Maybe our lives would have been easier if we didn't get the extension."

"Who promised us an easy life?" Roger said. "Bedtime, come here and snuggle with me."

Peggy was in deep thought when she said, "You know, hon, didn't you find it strange that Allie seemed to be sucking up to Andy and Laticia. I mean, like she knew they were engaged, and that 'you go girl' stuff, could that have been because Laticia 's Black?"

"That's enough! Come to bed, we need to celebrate it, not question our good fortune." And with that the two made love with great joy to celebrate their victory, but Peggy's observations were troublesome.

* * *

The whole team showed up the next day even though it wasn't a Monday, but they all agreed that they needed to chart a new path. Roger had them assembled in the conference room which had wall to wall whiteboards that had all been completely washed for their meeting. On a board on one wall he had the heading, *'What do we know?'* On another wall board he had *'What do we need to do?'* Roz stood at the boards ready to write down all the items yelled out to her.

"OK, guys, inventory time," Roger said

Andy was the first to start making a huge, convoluted statement about non-biologic diseases and especially those that might effect brain size. Roz asked, "Is that a *'Know'* or a *'Do'* item," she asked Andy.

"Both," he answered. "Is small brain size a pre-condition, or a symptom? We really do need to look into that."

"So, it's a *'Do'*" Roz said. "You know, of course, that it could just be a red herring that has absolutely nothing to do with DEF."

"Yes, but Andy's right. Until we do know then it's still something to be investigated," Ga Eun said.

And so the meeting went well into the evening when Roz sent out for pizzas. Around ten that night Roger called the meeting over. "That's it. I'm spent as I'm sure you all are too. We can continue with this tomorrow, but at some point we have to put this all into a plan to give Al, so I suggest that we wrap this part up ASAP. Peggy, Roz, and I will draft the plan based on what's up here. Nobody erase it! We'll all get together to finalize it later this week, OK?" Roger was smiling at all they had accomplished and knew that his team had done a yeoman's job to put all that info down on the wall.

Later that evening at home over a drink Roger said to Peggy, "I'm surprised we didn't get more inquiries about our work since the company's announcement. Do you think corporate news services might be preempting us from being bothered, or is the public just jaded?"

"I think Roz has done her job to keep us protected from the mob, so we need to be certain to thank her tomorrow."

* * *

However, on Wednesday more serious news came out about DEF. The CDC had new data on the affliction showing that deaths had more than doubled over the last month. Much of the data was felt to be based on a new awareness of DEF which led investigators to believe that many earlier causes attributed to Sudden Adult Death Syndrome (SADS) were actually caused by DEF. With this new revelation DEF was getting scarier causing the UN to hold a special session at its Manhattan Headquarters in two weeks.

"We've been invited by the Secretary General to make a presentation at that session, and I want you two there with me," Allen was telling Roger and Peggy over the phone.

"Could we bring the whole team with us?" Roger asked.

"No, no . . . that won't be necessary. We have just a twenty-minute window, so we'll give them just the bare bones presentation. The list of attendees reads like a who's who of the world scientific community. I suspect that we've been included because of the attention brought to your research by the press." Allen paused before adding, "OK, then, it's settled; it will be you, Peggie, me, and Allie. We'll meet on Thursday, August 7, for a run through; the meeting in New York is scheduled for the following Wednesday, that's the thirteenth, hope you're not superstitious," Allen said with a smile in his voice.

After they ended their call Peggy said, "I'm surprised that Allie didn't tell us to bring Andy and Laticia."

"OK, that's enough. We got work to do, so drop it with Allie already," Roger said in a brusque way.

* * *

On Monday, July 28, Andy was extremely irritable. "What's up, my friend?" Roger asked noticing Andy's uneasiness.

"DEF, that's what's up. At the rate it's increasing the entire world human population will be dead in less than three years and there is no sense of urgency. Holy shit, man we should all be off the wall with anxiety."

"And what exactly do you want the world to do? I think we all realize the importance of finding a cure, and hopefully we'll have solved the problem long before the *end of days*," Roger said slightly agitated at Andy's obvious impatience at getting rid of DEF.

"I don't know; I just hope that Al makes that point at next month's meeting. He has to tell the UN to jump in with both feet on this one and make them understand the full depth of the issue. If death rates keep doubling around every month or so since December then we've got just over two years left!

Two years! Holy shit, people, it's time to get our affairs in order."

"I can understand your anxiety . . ." Ga Eun said in a calm professional way, but Andy would have none of it.

"No! I don't think you can. I've waited a long time to find someone like Laticia, and now it looks like we won't be able to have kids, grow old together and do all the marvelous things that two people who love each other deeply might get out of life. How could you understand?"

"Andy, just because I've never actually married doesn't mean that I haven't had a love life. My partner and I have discussed this at some length, and we both sincerely believe that we will find a way out of it. Don't ask me how right now, but I think all of us feel what you and Laticia are going through. But if nothing else our work gives us hope that a solution is at hand. We all have to believe that or else we would just give up, and I, for one, am not ready to do that," Ga Eun said with such conviction that nobody spoke for a long time.

Finally, waiting for someone to break the silence Laticia said with tears in her voice, "Andy and I both want to thank you all for your love and support, and you need to forgive our impatience. We know that the world, and our group in particular, is wholeheartedly committed to . . . to finding a *solution* to DEF, but knowing the reality makes us very sad, so please, please let us do all we can to end this nightmare."

"Laticia, Andy, I promise you that we will, so let's get on with this meeting. Roger, What do we need to do for your UN presentation?" Roz asked, getting everyone back on message.

"Let's face it, we have just twenty minutes to show our results and Al will in all likelihood do the presentation. Not the best of circumstances to get our points across. Peggy and I will be there to answer any questions, most of which will probably be off the wall. I'm guessing that the meeting will be a lot of posturing to show that one's country is the best suited to do the work, but I'm hoping that an emergency group will be selected to actually do the work, and we'll be part of that group."

Looking at Andy, Roger continued. "I'm guessing that others are familiar with your doubling estimates, and they too will be bringing it up, but if they don't, we will. What we need are a couple of other talking points that will grab them and make them take serious actions like their lives depended on it, since it actually does."

The Narragansett DEF Group meeting became very animated with the entire group actively making suggestions what talking points needed to be brought up and then prioritizing them to insure that they got the biggest bang for their buck. They knew that Kolmogorov's influence would be marginal at best, so they had to make the most of it. By evening they felt that they were through preparing.

Andy's doubling issue of death rates was the highest priority if no one else brought it up first. Then, the issue of survival by family care, and finally the issue of climate change as the likely cause were the three highest priority points that needed to be made. If they were done convincingly enough then the group felt that the world's social, political, and scientific communities would come together to rid us of an immediate existential threat. And to do it in enough time to put DEF out of the picture and relegate it to other mass human extinction scenarios that never did come to fruition.

* * *

On Wednesday, August 13, 2031, The United Nations high-level meeting on DEF was held in the General Assembly hall with delegates from every member nation in attendance. The importance of the gathering was not lost on anyone present or the press from around the world. Kolmogorov

Industries was listed as eleventh to present, which put them in the spotlight at around the two PM window.

Presentations from WHO, CDC and comparable agencies from China, Russia, The United Kingdom, and France were all made in their allotted twenty-minute periods. Almost all of them simply raised the issue of how quickly DEF was spreading and that in less than three years, at current rates of infection, the world's population would be wiped out—action now was imperative!

No country gave any indication as to what they thought the syndrome was caused by, let alone any possible cure. But all agreed that it was not based on any known contagion, so any possible treatment, by necessity, remained elusive.

After the mid-afternoon break with presentations by a few private pharmaceutical corporations, and some smaller countries most of them proclaimed that with continued UN financial support they should be able to get results in a year or less. They actually believed that when no proven theories or treatment were known.

At a little after three in the afternoon Dr. Allen Phillip Morris, senior science officer at the United States Based Kolmogorov Industries was introduced. Allen had practiced his presentation to last fifteen minutes leaving some time for questions and had gone over it thoroughly with company based foreign language experts to make certain that nothing would be lost in translation; it was stunning.

"Members of the United Nations General Assembly, I come before you today to tell you that we have hope; hope to end this crisis and restore the world to a livable planet once again," Allen said in the clearest stentorian voice he could muster. He said it slowly and deliberately to ensure that the translators from around the world had enough time to do an accurate job. He had their attention.

After acknowledging the other presenters timeline to extinction he used Roger's example of coral polyps and bees as well-known species nearing extinction due to climate change. He then cited their as yet unpublished research on the finding of survivors who had been diagnosed with DEF but by having experienced significant love and care from their families and who had also experienced climatic environmental change incidents did survive.

Allen ended his presentation offering the services of his two senior researchers on the project to answer any technical questions in the time left allotted to him. But even more important, he told the assembly that Kolmogorov will self-finance all continuing research and not seek assistance from the UN or any other funding source. "It is our firm belief that we owe the world all we can do in our own house to rid us of this scourge, so we will not be seeking financial assistance to continue our quest to solve the DEF mystery. Furthermore, we welcome any member nation who wants to join in on our research the opportunity to work with us."

After an explosion of questions were shouted out the Secretary General banged his gavel and suggested that all questions to Kolmogorov be submitted in writing since it appears that the amount of interest would take us well into the night. There were still other organizations to be heard and in fairness to them he needed to curtail Kolmogorov's Q and A session. Allen promised that all questions will be answered as quickly as possible, but please be patient since it looks like there will be a lot of them.

At a little past 3:30 the session was brought to order again and the rest of the speakers presented their thoughts. None were anywhere near as explosive as Kolmogorov's. Most of the twelve remaining presenters spent their shortened time claiming that Kolmogorov's presentation was a game changer and they wished to be part of their team.

Allen Morris, but not Peggy and Roger, nor for that matter Allie were invited to dinner with the Secretary General, and the senior delegates from the five permanent members of the security council. It was quite a night for the Kolmogorov's DEF team, and they all were delighted by the news that they were the de facto lead DEF investigators in the world.

CHAPTER SEVEN

The next two weeks were a whirlwind of activity and change. All calls concerning DEF were automatically transferred directly to corporate, and the six researchers in the DEF Group were given new untraceable cell phones. Allen wanted them to move their South Kingston operation to Providence, but they all agreed that it would be like moving into a zoo. So, instead of moving, heavy 24/7 security was added to their facility and the South Kingston police also kept an eye out for any unusual traffic heading towards their facility. Roz had it hardest guarding the front door from unwanted visitors and told Roger she wished he'd reconsider moving to the Providence site for safety and security reasons. But Roger stayed firm in wanting to continue the DEF study in Narragansett.

On Thursday, September 25, Roger got a call from Ga Eun's partner that Ga Eun had died. It seemed that she became ill last Tuesday and was taken to the hospital on Thursday, the eighteenth where she quickly deteriorated and died. Only Roger and Peggy from the group had ever met Ga Eun's partner. She contacted Roger using Ga Eun's work phone to tell him of her passing; the preliminary diagnosis was DEF. Needless to say that everyone was shocked and extremely upset at the news of Ga Eun's totally unexpected death

Roger contacted the rest of the team directly to tell them of their colleagues loss. They all showed up on Friday morning to commiserate with each other. "I hope the funeral doesn't turn into a media circus," Andy said but Roz admonished him.

"Jesus, Andy, who gives a shit about the media. Aren't you the least bit saddened by Ga Eun's dying? Roz asked.

"Oh, for God's sake, Roz, of course I am. I'm just hoping that she'd be remembered in a dignified way, but I just know that won't happen once the media prints the story; 'DEF researcher dies from DEF.' We all loved Ga Eun, and speaking for Laticia too, we're gonna miss her greatly," Andy answered in a sincere way.

"The funeral is next week in order to give all her family time to come to Providence for the funeral. I'm assuming that we'll all be there," Peggy said.

"Where are they coming from?" Laticia asked.

"Mostly California, that's where she's originally from. They plan on taking her body back to San Francisco after the ceremony here. Angela, Ga Eun's partner, is making all the arrangements and will keep us informed."

"OK, we all need to do whatever we think is appropriate, but I think we should dedicate ourselves even harder to getting the job done for Ga Eun's sake. Monday is an important meeting with Al and his crew filling us in on all our new national and international partners. They whittled the list down to five other organizations, but there's tons of others on the 'keep informed' list. We'll see you all Monday," Roger said, somewhat abruptly ending the ad hoc meeting.

* * *

On Monday morning Allen started the meeting by offering his sincere condolences to Ga Eun's family and colleagues and urged us to remember her by working extra hard to rid the world of DEF. It was sadly trite and rather emotionless, but for Allen it was the best he could do.

Peggy replied to Allen's remark, "Thanks, Al, and yes, we have already dedicated ourselves to Ga Eun's memory. She was an important part of this team and we'll be lost without her."

After a few seconds of silence Allen introduced them to their new partners and set up working parameters—who reported to whom, where and how future meetings would be held—and other organizational considerations were laid out. The five institutes chosen as partners were the cream of United States and European research and development institutions, as well as governmental organizations. The CDC and The World Health Organization (WHO) were the first two, and Johns Hopkins University Dept. of Molecular Biology was next even though they all knew that DEF was not a transmissible disease.

But the fact that death is considered a medical condition it would be those public and private organizations, like Johns Hopkins, as the most capable of offering the expertise they might need in their medical efforts. MIT and the European Centre for Disease Prevention and Control rounded out the team.

It looked like MIT was the only non-strictly medically based organization, but there were several other organizations (primarily non-English speaking) who were to be kept informed and asked to offer any advice they saw fit. When the Zoom meeting ended Roger's team was exhausted. But the real bomb came when Andy and Laticia later that day informed Roger, Peggy, and Roz that they were moving on.

Andy was moving to corporate and was taken Laticia with him as his aide. They would be moving out by the end of October, but Andy felt that after seeing the make-up of Kolmogorov's collaborators from the science and information community he felt that his presence was no longer necessary.

"Look, you know I love you guys, and now I'll be in a much better place to help you get the job done. I've been promised that I could stay involved as much as you want from me, and Laticia here will keep us focused on the humanistic side of the problem. Hey, it's a win-win situation. The DEF team will have us in senior management, and you, Roger, will still have Peggy and Roz, the three most important people left on the project. I think you'll be busy enough keeping all the egos of your new partners on point without having to put up with me, so any way . . . not much else I can say," Andy said, deeply saddened by his own announcement.

"Roz, I hope you're not planning on leaving us too are you?" Peggy asked. Roz replied that in no uncertain terms would she leave now that they seemed so close to success.

* * *

In early October the DEF team, or what was left of them, of Roz, Roger and Peggy quietly moved back to Roger's and Peggy's house on Perkins Avenue. Now most of their time was spent on Zoom calls bringing their partners up to date on their research and what others were doing. Their work on climate change, in particular, was the most sought after by the major institutions.

But it turned out later in the month, that a small facility in Brazil known to be a leader in human ecology was a 'keep informed' organization. They were engaged in the study of the effects that family relations had on an individual's wellbeing, and they invited the DEF team to visit them.

"I'm glad Laticia is going with us to Brazil. After all, it was mostly her digging into Andy's data that laid the groundwork for our theory," Peggy was saying as they were packing their bags for their trip to South America.

Roger said, "I'm surprised that Andy doesn't want to go too. I would hope that top management would be interested in being in on this work. Hey, but it's their call. I'm only glad that Al has not asked us to take Allie along."

The Instituto Nacional de Humanismo Ecologica was a small university by national standards, with only 12,000 students and staff but had an excellent international reputation. Located on a beautiful campus in Curitiba, Brazil, the end of October put it right in the middle of spring. The three Americans were put up in guest faculty housing and treated royally. Their host was an ex-pat American educated in the states as an Urban Geographer who headed up their environmental adaptations studies.

Jacob "Jake" Donald Rothstein was fifty-four-years-old and still mostly trim with the exception of a little middle age bump. He was a full professor of human ecology who spoke fluent Portuguese along with his native English which he was delighted to use again speaking with his American guests.

"Yes, I was educated at Michigan in their Geology Department where I got my Ph.D. in 2000—they had already deep sixed their geography department. You know that Michigan was a leader in human ecology back in the 1940s and 50s with Rob McKenzie and his student Amos Hawley. Their work in Sociology laid the foundation for my work as an urban geographer. I was more quantitative than the other soc guys, but they liked my work. Anyway, when I heard about you guys seeing climate as the cause of DEF, and a possible treatment through human interaction, well I had to jump on board," Jake said.

Laticia, as the team's ethnologist, filled Jake in on her findings, but credited her results to the excellent data analyses Andy performed. "Without his digging into the data to seek out the possible relevant variables there was no way I would ever have found it," she explained.

"Yeah, similarly if it wasn't for Peggy's earlier data enquiries I, too, probably wouldn't have found the global warming connection," Roger said.

"But your people found it, and that's all that counts now. The next question is, what are you going to do with it? And if you haven't gotten that far yet, then I would love to help out in that quest," Jake said.

And so a new collaboration was started with Jake's team of junior faculty and grad students. Working with Kolmogorov's DEF team it proved to be the winning combination in the world's search for a DEF solution.

* * *

With the world death total at around 15,000, it still wasn't considered an epidemic, let alone a pandemic, but with doubling time under two months epidemiologists were genuinely concerned. Andy's earlier comments about everyone would be dead in three years was on target and that meant that only two years was actually left to get the job done. It was time to panic.

On Monday, November 24, 2031, three days before Thanksgiving, the DEF team met with Jake on a Zoom call. "Wow, that was quick. It's like we just got back and already you have some results? What's up?" Peggy asked.

"Intervening variables, that's what's up," Jake said.

"Huh? Where?" Laticia asked. She had requested to stay and work with the DEF team but would be reporting to Andy and could be pulled at any time if she was needed elsewhere.

Intervening variables, sometimes called mediating variables, are frequently found between a dependent and an independent variable. In the current case, DEF is the dependent variable and 'family care' is an independent one. But for causal relations to be assumed the researcher must rule out any other variable or set of variables that could cause the outcome.

"Are you saying that Andy neglected some important factors; I don't think so . . ." Laticia started to say when Jake cut in.

"No, no . . . on the contrary. Andy's factor analysis was superb as any outstanding statistician like Andy's would be. But you Laticia, who is more trained as a sociologist should know that the numbers aren't all that clear cut when dealing with people's habitat. Our team here looked at other variables besides the ones that you and Andy came up with and found that although it's true the family factor had the highest correlation, it also had a lot of cross correlation with other indexes leading us to believe that some of these might be just as significant as the family variable you produced," Jake explained.

"What were those, Jake?" Roger asked anxiously.

"Right," Jake said anxious to continue his presentation. "And so we've concluded that three of these are really intervening variables, and they're not the usual demographic suspects like wealth, education, sex or age, and the like. No, these three are most unusual. But our research into human ecology has led us to look at more place related factors. The three factors we linked are 'living arrangements,' and the other two are ones my earliest ecology professor told me about when she said, 'It's all about feeding and fucking,'" Jake said.

After a few seconds to digest Jake's premise Peggy said in an offhanded way, "I'm guessing that feeding and fucking are also closely correlated with living arrangements."

"Yes, of course. All are co-dependent, but more importantly I think we may have a handle on how to treat DEF patients who are still alive," Jake said ignoring Peggy's attempt at humor.

"I don't even want to guess how you came up with your treatment but what is it?" Roger asked.

"Well, first of all we know that DEF, by the way, we should look into getting that name changed—anyhow, it's climate induced stress, right? And until recently we thought it was always fatal. We also know that those who died had a smaller than average brain size, but we knew nothing of their character traits," Jake explained before adding, "By the way, the smaller brain size we found was attributed to the hardly noticeable smaller than average weight of the frontal lobe, the center that controls personality."

"So, what does all that have to do with treating those who have it, but aren't dead yet?" Peggy asked.

"Be patient, I'm getting to that. What I need to tell you is that we were able to do a character analysis of those who we know survived in their isolated communities and found that they all had mostly passed the age of character growth, or puberty, and all were classified as the loveable, jocular type. You know what I mean, the guys and gals called 'happy-go-lucky,' always had a joke on their tongues and a smile on their face. The kind that every clique had and protected, even though they were usually the butt of their jokes and the ones to suffer ridicule." Jake paused for a few seconds before going on. "It looks like they got even. While the rest of us are dying off, they're the ones surviving."

"But how does that tie into your cure and the three variables you told us about?" Laticia asked.

"Yeah, yeah, I'm getting to that. These character types are also the most likely to be loved by their families or care givers and given the best home environments. Food, and nutrition would be part of that, and of course lots of sexual activity after leaving home. It was these factors that protected them from climate induced stress. But the added knowledge that they, or their families, had migrated from regions currently having mostly stable environments to . . . well, to almost anywhere in the world today that's currently undergoing severe climate disruptions."

"How does that come into play? I mean, almost the entire world human population came from relatively stable environments and are now living in shit, so how does that set them apart?" Roger wanted to know.

"Yeah, that was the tough one. But first of all I need to point out that living in a shitty place, as you put it, is not new. Human settlements have cropped up in all sorts of severe climates, but it's not the climate that's stressing them out, it's the change in climate. Anyway, we're thinking forward genetic pressures might be in play here. Evolution had somehow selected them to be better equipped to survive based on character traits that mostly evolved from people who were the staid and no-nonsense types, who were forced for various reasons to leave their places of origin. That happy-go-lucky attitude, or gene mutation, seems to be the driver."

Nobody talked for about a minute before Roger jumped in and asked again, "Jake, all that is fascinating, but I don't see a treatment in there yet. More important, I'm still confused as to how you're going to figure out who has DEF—or whatever it's called in the future—and treat them. I mean, if we all agree it's primarily a climate related stress, well that won't end for at least another generation or longer. There's no time for that to happen before annihilation."

"Yes, and that's what I'm about to tell you. The good news is we don't have to wait until the global warming crisis is turned back in order to save us. We have developed an intervention strategy that could save the world," Jake said shocking all the others into silence, while Jake explained.

* * *

"Do you think he's got it right? I mean, gene therapy? Splicing the genes of those survivors into those affected?" Laticia asked after they finished their meeting with Jake.

"I don't think it's a splice job so much as a gene modification like the mRNA process used in vaccine making. Even if he is telling us it's like a vaccine, it would be damned near impossible to do that on the scale required to save us all. I think that Jake is too far removed from reality to help us here. I know, he sounds rational and all, but to inoculate almost the entire world population? I think he needs to present his argument to our other partners and let them all in before we make any draconian recommendations like that. Anyway, we need to bounce it off of our own bosses here at Kolmogorov," Roger said and then asked Laticia, "Laticia, would you ask Andy to set that up for us?"

The day before Thanksgiving, Allen had the DEF team come into Providence to tell his staff what Jake recommended. Andy was there representing corporate management and Allie Ginsburg was the first to comment after Roger and Peggy's presentation.

"So he wants to make the world into a bunch of doofuses . . . a bunch of Cosmo Kramers. No, I don't think we can, or should support that." Allie was referring to the character on the old Seinfeld show still in re-runs. But Kramer was not at all the type of person that fitted Jake's description.

"I don't think Kramer captures what Jake was referring to. His character descriptor was of someone who is happy and fun to be around, not a stupid person, or an incompetent one," Laticia offered, not intimidated by Allie's authority in Allen's group.

"It doesn't matter who Jake was describing. Trying to change the world's entire genetic structure of humans is simply out to the question . . ." Allen started to say when Andy interrupted.

"Yes, that may be true, but letting the human race die off in a year or two is not a good choice either. I think we need to bring it up with our partners for discussion and we need to bring in ethicists and religious leaders as well."

And that was it. The future head of Kolmogorov Industries had spoken. An international meeting, jointly sponsored by the UN's WHO and co-chaired by Kolmogorov Industries and The Instituto Nacional de Humanismo Ecologica was scheduled for mid-December in the Hague's Peace Palace.

* * *

By the time the meeting started it was estimated that almost a half-million people had died from DEF and the world was operating in panic mode. Every country, every village, every outpost in the world seemed to be affected and people were demanding that their governments and the UN start doing something *NOW!* The secretary general gaveled the meeting to order on an unusually snowy day in The Hague.

"Maybe the weather is a sign of our challenge—unexpected difficulties. Or maybe it's a portent of good things coming—global cooling. Whatever it is today we will be offered a potential way out of the current DEF crisis, while we are still trying to come out of the original crisis that led to this one, climate change. I urge this body to pay close attention to our esteemed colleagues from the United States and Brazil. Don't be skeptical, nor dismissive out of hand, but keep an open mind, and be aware of the existential threat that is now less than two years away." Here she paused. Looking around the huge, ornate room she continued.

"The hope of the world is truly on your shoulders so please deliberate carefully and then present the world with a consensual strategy to end DEF—that is as consensual as practicable with such diverse interests and outlooks as are represented here."

At this point she turned the meeting over to Jake and Allen while their senior staff sat close by to field any requests that either one might ask of them. After Allen reiterated Kolmogorov's findings about DEF and briefly reviewed their subsequent work with Jake he let Jake make his presentation.

During Jake's talk lots of the almost one-hundred participants remained quiet and listened, occasionally looking at their handouts written in English, Portuguese, and their native language. The handouts were summaries of the extensive graphs and charts that Jake was now presenting in detail. After Jake finished, about an hour into the conference, the secretary announced a break to let everyone digest Jake's proposed solution before continuing. After the break, and still about an hour or so before lunch the real fun began.

* * *

"Wow!" That was some shit storm! But delighted the way you managed it Jake," Roger said to Jake after the meeting ended.

"They just needed to understand that mRNA treatments are well suited to modify harmful genes, but not affect the patient's behavior. It surprised me that I had to tell them about what a one-to-many mapping was, and that by just changing one gene in a complex behavioral process rarely affected the entire process . . ."

"You're preaching to the choir, Jake," Peggy said, "I was as surprised as you that so many raised the specter of genetically modified foods as akin to what you were proposing."

"Didn't surprise me at all," Allen said. "After the way my own staff initially reacted I expected it, but glad you were there to explain it so nicely, Jake. Anyway, when do you think we can start clinical trials?"

"Are we assuming here that mRNA technology like the Covid vaccine will work without first testing on animals?" Roger asked.

"No reason to believe otherwise," Jake said. "We've already done a few small animal studies on the DEF gene just to assess safety concerns and they proved safe."

"So, you've already named it the DEF gene. I thought that we wanted to change the DEF designation for our disorder," Peggy observed.

"Just temporary, Peggy, until we get some international standards group to come up with an official designation," Jake answered.

"Whatever! Let's stick to business here. I repeat, when can we start clinical trials in people?" Allen persisted.

"Tomorrow," Jake said, which shocked them all. "We've already selected over 30,000 subjects around the world that would be willing to participate, and all we need is one of our partners, say Pfizer, to produce the materials. With a balls out effort we should be in business in under a month."

"I'll get right on it," Allen said. "Remember everyone, we're doing this for Ga Eun."

CHAPTER EIGHT

They expected anywhere from 20 to 40 deaths due to DEF would be recorded during the testing period in an untreated adult (15 to 60 years old) population of 30,000. But in the treated group no deaths were attributed to DEF. All the deaths that did occur were attributed to known causes.

The public waited in great anticipation for the results of the DEF vaccine, as the press had labeled it, even though it was in no way a vaccine in the clinical sense. From a statistical viewpoint the treatment was an enormous success. Now the problem would be treating the whole world with gene modification technology. That, as was expected, was a problem, but a doable one.

WHO, along with major health agencies like CDC in the United States, and governmental organizations around the world got into high gear with the intent to treat every man woman and child by the end of 2032, regardless of their current genetic situation.

And they accomplished it!

Well, at least they thought they had. But in certain remote areas of the world, like jungle regions in South America, and some Indigenous Peoples' villages in the arctic, small populations were bypassed. Where communication between those places and the developed world were supported, efforts were made to treat them, but lots of those populations chose not to be treated.

By early 2033 deaths attributed to DEF were almost non-existent, and like the Covid pandemic the world, once again, congratulated itself on choosing science-based decision making over irrational choices to, once again, save the planet. With climate change also getting under control the Earth was saved for all its inhabitants for the foreseeable future, and that was a good thing.

Except for one thing, a certain strain of cancer that was once thought to be mostly non-fatal was beginning to show up in unusually larger than expected numbers. And this time, it proved to be extremely fatal.

* * *

"It turns out that the gene we modified to cure DEF was probably a tumor-suppressant-gene responsible for keeping Merkel Cell Carcinoma from so aggressively going fatal. But that's all speculation. Anyway, I'm worried since just about the entire world population has had that gene altered," Jake was explaining to the Kolmogorov DEF team on a Zoom meeting in June of 2033.

"Do you have any idea how we can prevent it? If it's simply skin cancer isn't that relatively easy to treat?" Peggy asked.

"Well, yes. Most treated skin cancers have a five-year survival rate of almost eighty per cent, but in the cases that are being reported now the survival rate for even six months after diagnosis is almost zero. That makes it a new and totally unknown cancer mechanism out there. Or, just as likely a new and unknown human genetic response to cancer. I'm betting on the latter," Jake said.

"Holly shit! Can we do another gene modification treatment? I mean, is that it; is it over for us this time?" Roger asked.

"I wish I knew Roger. The gene we altered can't be re-modified back, if that's what you mean, and to try and develop another gene to replace it, well that's going to be difficult since for all practical purposes that gene, in its original form, is out of the gene pool. I think we're stuck with finding a cure for Merkel Cell. I think we need to have the entire team in on this one. Can you have Andy do another end-of-the-world calculation? That should get their attention," Jake said noticeably upset by his own report.

"We'll get right on it, Jake. In the meantime you should make your results known to the world scientific community as soon as you can," Laticia said.

"You should also let the world know what symptoms they need to be looking out for and start getting help ASAP if they spot em," Roz interjected, something she rarely did at these meetings.

After Jake signed off the DEF team knew that they had to tell Allen and Andy at once. What Jake told them at first stunned them into inaction at the new challenge they faced.

"What are you thinking?" Roger asked Peggy.

"Maybe that old advertisement bromide about not fooling with mother nature was truer than we realized. Maybe we should have waited longer to see the results of the study before doing a GMO trip on the entire world's human population. I don't know, shit! I really think that this time we're fucked."

* * *

Peggy knew that sometimes the ideas and theories of some people were smarter and farther reaching than the original thinkers ever could realize. Not messing with nature was probably another one of those ideas. Climate change was probably the costliest, at least to date, of an outcome that carried far more consequences than was ever expected. Now, however, humans had really messed up this time by disrupting one of the most robust survival mechanisms found in nature: DNA.

It wasn't long before the rest of the world was sadly aware of what they had done and was scrambling like never before to fix it. All sorts of crackpot theories were postulated as fixes for the new, and this time very real, end of the world scenario. People were grasping at all sorts of scams around the globe and taking all kinds of things into their bodies, paying exorbitant prices, only to die off like the rest of their neighbors. Even the legitimate scientific community was at a standstill from preventing certain death to all those treated for DEF.

By early summer of 2033, sadly Peggy and Roger were in the early wave of deaths since they were near the first to get the treatment. They were back at Roger's family home in Michigan where they died a few days apart thankful that they didn't have children to either watch them die, or for them to watch perish.

Laticia and Andrew were also early to go shortly after they had gone back to Andrew's parents' house. They, too were grateful that they hadn't started a family yet. Roz was the last to pass, all alone in her apartment with nobody around to witness it or comfort her in the end.

Scenes not seen since the bubonic plague of the 1300s, that killed off a third of Europe and at least as many in other parts of the world were played out. Bodies piled up in morgues, on streets, in homes; the smell of death was all around for the carrion eater's to savor. It was civilization's worst nightmare, and it was happening the world over as if nature was finally getting even with humans for their wanton treatment of the Earth's environment. The silence in the great cities was palpable with the exception of the flesh eaters scavenging for whatever was left for them to take leaving nothing but bones as evidence of who once lived there.

The UN, or rather, what was left of the UN could do nothing to prevent the inevitable outcome while the world's DEF treated population became decimated in less than a year by Merkel Cell Carcinoma. Since well over 99% of the world's population had been treated by the end of 2032, by Christmas 2033, there was nobody left to celebrate the holiday. The few people that weren't killed off by carcinoma eventually succumbed to DEF, so the devastation was complete.

The animals, domesticated and wild for all intents and purposes, took over the earth as death spread through the world.

* * *

However in some isolated places on the planet and in some Indigenous Peoples' habitats, humans had survived.

The question as to how these primitive, unsophisticated, yet mostly happy-go-lucky people could somehow or other eventually repopulate the entire Earth remained unanswered. And if they did, would they want to restart the technological conquest of the world, an epoch hundreds of years in its making? Would these survivors go on to reclaim the world as a mostly human settlement for highly skilled, highly educated and highly motivated beings? In fact, could that ever happen again?

If history is a clue to answer those questions, then it should be noted that some species on the verge of extinction have been brought back from the brink. But not without tremendous human, or divine, intervention being the driving force for their survival. Without such intervention and the willingness of some power to grant the species a pardon it was highly doubtful humans would come back to anywhere near their place in history. A place where they were once such a hugely creative, and simultaneously totally destructive force. Only time would tell, but in the meantime this is what happened after the world ending die out of 2033.

* * *

On a beautiful day, July 15, 2034, (mid-winter in the south pacific) in an extremely remote Melanesian Indigenous Peoples' community called Waitara one such primitive group had discovered the death of the outside world. Waitara, which translates to "clean water mountain stream," was located near the village of Aneghowhat on Aneityum island, Vanuatu. Osh, a highly respected member of the community, returned from his fifty mile by sea annual trip to Lenakel village on Tanna island, due north of Aneityum. He was very distraught when he told his extended family the news that everybody on Lenakel was dead.

"What did you see, Osh?" His cousin asked.

"I saw death! The animals had eaten most dead people. They had been dead for many days. I had to fight off the dogs with sticks, but lots of animals—chickens, pigs—were dead too. It is a place of death that we must never go to anymore. We are completely by ourselves now for living and other worldly goods. That is what I saw," he said.

"What killed them?" his eldest son, Kaikoa, asked.

"I don't know. There were none left with visible scars, or other signs that would tell me what they died from, but I do know that it must have been fast, days, weeks at most. All their possessions—guns, boats—were still there untouched, and I believe, still in good working order. I don't understand why they didn't leave."

"Did you bring anything back with you?" Kaikoa wanted to know.

"No! It was all filled with death so I did not touch anything that I could avoid. I washed vigorously before getting back in my boat to come home. I hope that I have not brought anything with me that would harm our people," he said with deep concern in his voice.

"Did you stop at Aneghowhat to tell them what you saw?" his wife asked.

"No, I came the same way that I left down the river without going through the village. I don't like the people there, and I don't trust them, so I did not stop," he replied.

Osh's people were descendants of Indigenous Peoples whose ancestry went back thousands of years, or maybe even longer. They still lived in primitive dwellings fed by an abundance of fruits and vegetables, and a clean water stream. They also farmed pigs and chickens brought to the island by their ancestors many hundreds of years earlier.

Osh, a gifted sailor, made his annual wintertime eight hour, fifty-mile ocean trip in an outrigger canoe with a sail. In their winter, the weather was drier and the ocean calmer making for safer travel. He navigated to the village of Lanakel on the island of Tanna north of Aneityum. He kept his home's location on Aneityum island unknown from the people of Lenakel, who just assumed he was a spice farmer from Aneityum who preferred doing business in their spice market rather than in the markets on his island.

At that time of year, when it was winter in Vanuatu, it was summer in the northern hemisphere. The skies over Vanuatu would be visited by a number of airplanes flying out of Port Vila, Vanuatu's capital city airport, located two-hundred miles to the north of Aneityum. Small planes carried visitors from the northern climes to the far southern islands of Vanuatu to spend cooler mid-summer vacation trips in that area of the South Pacific.

Even on the remotest inhabited island in the Vanuatu chain, Aneityum, the occasional plane could be seen just to the south of Osh's community landing on Mystery Island. The low flying planes were a source of curiosity to the inhabitants who wondered why planes never landed in their compound. It was probably because nobody else in the world knew where Waitara was, let alone know if they could even land a plane there.

After a lot of talk and confusion from his family as to what they should do with the information Osh brought back from Lenakel they decided they had to inform the elders of the community. The startling news led the elders to authorize Osh to take four other members of the community's smartest and bravest young people and go to Aneghowhat and tell the people what he found in Lenakel. The residents of Aneghowhat may not have been the most civil people to members of the Waitara Community, but they never harmed them and, for the most part, had let them live in peace in their isolated and difficult to reach settlement.

And so it was agreed that the fisherman Osh, his son Kaikoa, and another young man, Ruru, along with two young women, Mea, and Anuhea, would go into Aneghowhat village. There they would seek out the local police office and tell them what Osh discovered in Lenakel.

The selected group of envoys all spoke French as well as Bislama, the local tribal language, but more importantly they were not afraid to leave their secret area to visit another part of the island even if it wasn't always a hospitable place for them.

* * *

Waitara, the clearing where the Osh's family lived, went through countless changes due to volcanic activity and other seismic upheavals. But the people of the original tribe that migrated, in all likelihood, from Africa, remained and kept rebuilding over the centuries of natural disasters. Lifestyle changes were experienced when the occasional migrant brought in cultural modifications, like educational standards and work equality for all members including women, and gay, and lesbian members of the group. These new attributes slowly evolved the social make-up of the tribe and prepared them for isolation and survival.

The people of Waitara were a happy and joyful group with a quick wit and a hard to anger mentality. Almost all of them possessed a wry sense of humor that mixed reality with fantasy, but they had little need for an organized religion. They had few ceremonial events, births, deaths, and marriages were three of them. And they did believe that their dead ancestors somehow guided them, but they did not hold to a concept of a belief in an all-powerful god.

A couple of hundred years earlier a French missionary found their community and with his bible he taught them to read French. But as for their conversion to Christianity that didn't go over very well, so he left after years of trying to convince them of a Christian God's existence. But they did like to speak French so that was incorporated into their culture, but no god-like being was adopted.

The community's population never exceeded more than a couple of thousand members and with outmigration rare, a population of around a thousand had been stable for centuries with a life expectancy of around 65 years. The major causes of death were accidents and local diseases, making death rates and birth rates almost the same. Government was by consensus, but elders were respected for preserving the community's institutional memory and their closeness to their ancestors. The elders were also responsible for sanctioning the little business with the outside world that the tribe was engaged in, like the one Osh conducted in Lenakel trading spices for metal utensils and tools.

So, on July 16, the four young people from the community, led by Osh, put on their best T-shirts, sarongs, and sandals, and marched unafraid into Aneghowhat. It was not long before the party realized that what Osh saw on the island to the north was the same for Aneghowhat—total death.

"Don't touch anything," Osh said to his team, "This may be some kind of plague that we know nothing about. We must all wash fully before going back home."

Kaikoa and Ruru wanted to stay behind to study the situation further, but Osh told them that they couldn't do that yet. The two young men were informed by Osh that, "We need more guidance from our elders as to what our next action should be."

It would take a full week of discussions, deliberations, and the need to overcome distrust of the unknown before a decision was made. Tribal ceremonies and other civil functions had been curtailed during the southern hemisphere winter and dry season while the issue of so many dead people in the world was being dealt with. Unrest was being felt in the community and a lot of citizens just wanted to return to their normal routines and not concern themselves with the death of other people.

"We have not been victims of the affliction and we have walked among them. I think it's time we began to celebrate our new freedom from the outside and live like we have since the beginning of time. We have all the food we need, and we can make all the clothes and houses we want, so let us get on with our lives," an elder proposed at their monthly, full moon all person's council meeting to much foot stomping, dancing, and singing.

And so it was done. It was agreed that they would no longer make trips out of the community and live as they had for centuries before contact with the outside world was made. But there were four people who did not agree with that, however they did not say anything at that time. It would be months before their insubordination was discovered.

* * *

For four months, until the end of November, a few weeks before the hot rainy season started in December, two men, Kaikoa and Ruru, and two women, Mea and Anuhea would go unnoticed back into the village of Aneghowhat. They rummaged through buildings and houses for anything new and interesting trying to understand their purpose. But they didn't take anything back with them for fear of bringing death to their community. At first clothing seemed to interest them along with kitchen items.

"Mea, what do you think this could be used for?" Anuhea asked holding up a grater on a recent trip into the village.

"Let me see," Mea said while closely examining the kitchen appliance. "Ho! The holes are sharp! They cut easily. Maybe it is used to make copra flour," examining the device very carefully.

"Hmm, I don't think so. You would need to cut the copra into small pieces. I think we should look for other things that we could figure out," Anuhea said.

But what really interested Anuhea was books. She had seen a book used by an elder woman who performed certain rituals during ceremonies, and as small children they even learned the French alphabet. But with nothing to read, they were never taught how to read simply because there was no need for it. But now, seeing books, newspapers, magazines many in different alphabets her curiosity was really piqued. At first she was attracted to magazines with lots of strange and extremely interesting pictures and she tried very hard to discern the meanings of the captions.

"My father Osh knows how to understand the letters," Kaikoa said as he watched Anuhea, who happened to be his fiancé, look through the magazines.

"Do you think he'd teach us?" she asked eagerly.

"Yes, I'm sure he would. He tried to teach me, but without much to look at I lost interest. Let me see if I can still understand how it's done," he said as he looked at a two-and-a-half-year-old January 22, 2032, issue of Paris Match.

After he carefully parsed out each word on the cover Anuhea translated what she heard Kaikoa read in stumbling French, "The New Life," she said excitedly as she heard Kaikoa say, *"La Nouvelle Vie."*

They smiled at their discovery and so it began, that singular event on that sun drenched late spring day in November, an event that would change their lives, and the world's future to a less uncertain outcome.

* * *

When Kaikoa told his father what he and his friends had done, Osh straightaway notified the elders. The elders agreed to allow the young people's petition to bring some of the books to the community after they acknowledged their inappropriate activities over the previous four months.

The citizens of Waitara were quite permissive allowing their young people to do pretty much what they wanted. So, after hearing that they had been going to Aneghowhat for four months without any ill effects they agreed to let them bring their books back to share with the community.

That simple act led to the community's very first library, and their school would now teach reading in earnest. The most popular books requested were French to Bislama dictionaries

102

followed by books on engineering and medicine. In two years the vast majority of Waitara's young people between the ages of five and twenty knew how to read. As the community's knowledge increased the desire to travel to other places among the younger generation grew.

First there were trips to other villages on the island where other discoveries like motorized boats and electric motors were discovered and taken apart to learn how they worked.

Mea became a master engineer who had a voracious appetite for all things mechanical and electrical. With her skill and knowledge she taught other interested youths and together they restored the very primitive, but effective electric grid in Aneghowhat which dazzled the other community members. Also, within just four years of discovery of, what was to them, modern science a number of citizens took up residence in Aneghowhat, the former largest village on the island.

But what really started them on the road to discovery was finding the airplane on Mystery Island still intact and able to fly. It took two sixteen-year old's just four months of research to learn how to fuel and fly the plane. Soon, navigation by instruments was mastered and sea travel followed—they were off to the races.

If the Earth's left-over infrastructure could start up again with the right people at the helm and without war, famine, and global warming, then even the sky wasn't the limit. Just as the world had recovered from the loss of dinosaurs and over 70% of all the world's species millions of years earlier, so would it recover from the loss of over 99% of its human population in 2033.

CHAPTER NINE

By the year 2050, or a half generation after the introduction of universal literacy into the lives of Waitara's citizens, remarkable changes had occurred. Travel had expanded by diesel powered ships and small planes to Port Villa, the capital on Efate island, two hundred miles to the north. Trips to the capital city was an awe-inspiring event and the entire population was urged to visit to see what they now had at their disposal.

The people of Waitara had no currency or means of exchange for acquiring property or other possessions. Each individual had essentially nothing, yet each had everything they needed. Food, clothing, shelter, entertainment were all shared and each person contributed to these necessities of life for themselves and other members of the community. Some had specialties, like Osh as a fisherman and Ruru as a musician, but they too helped out at harvest time, cooking communal meals, and home building. But with knowledge from books and travel lifestyles changed.

The government of Waitara had also changed with the addition of three new ministries: The Ministry of Science and Education, the Ministry of Arts and Music, and the Ministry of Justice. Osh, at 67, was now an elder and was selected by the other elders as their leader. His knowledge of the other islands and his ability to read and navigate was the reason he was chosen. But it was because of his wisdom and judgement that he was treasured by the entire community.

Mea was a natural to become the Minister of Science and Education, Ruru took over the Ministry of Arts and Music, while both Kaikoa and Anuhea were chosen to run Justice as co-chief ministers. The community never had a need for a justice department, but since the introduction of vastly different and valuable possessions came into the community, decisions over ownership and access began to arise with the occasional outbreak of violence. Violent acts against citizens was an extremely rare event up until around ten years ago when travel and education began in earnest. Some had warned that this would happen, but so much had changed since the loss of so many other people in the world they knew that change in their lives would be inevitable.

* * *

One afternoon, while reading poetry, Kaikoa asked Anuhea, "What do you think the poet, Eliot, meant by our world ending, 'Not with a bang, but a whimper?'".

"I think the bang was referring to war, but the whimper, a weak cry, is lost on me. Why do you ask?"

"I don't know. I was just reading him, and it occurred to me that I didn't fully understand it. In any case, our world will not end, and certainly if it does it will not be with a *whimper*," Kaikoa said.

After being lost in thought for a moment he continued, "I think that maybe our people were chosen by our ancestors to find any others still out there and make the world over again. But this time we will not destroy the air we breathe nor the water we drink, both of which brings life and comfort to all that live. We will not do as the others who have perished did. I think that is why their ancestors took the world away from them and told our ancestors to give it back to us."

"I think you are a born philosopher and I love you very much but come it's time for the council meeting," Anuhea said.

It was at the monthly council meeting in February 2051, where Mea began her latest pitch on expanding their boundaries. "Because we will eventually run out of fuel and we are in no position to develop such an industry on our own," Mea was telling the council of elders, "that is why we need to pursue other ways to use the world's left-over resources."

"So, what is it you are proposing we do?" Osh asked.

"Oh, where to start. First of all we have to revive something called the internet, or the World-Wide-Web, then we need to train everyone how to use it, and then we need to develop solar and nuclear energy sources to power all our devices for living . . ."

"What devices are you talking about? We have all the food and water we need, all the building and clothing materials for our bodies and houses. What else do we need? Yes, yes, Ruru has discovered new music making devices, but we still dance and sing to the same tunes. But we also have all the resources that the others left behind when they left this world. And most importantly, we have new ways to gain knowledge, with much thanks to you. I just don't understand why the insistence on making everything here in Waitara like it was on the rest of the planet before the plague."

"Father is right," Kaikoa said, "we are a people of merely a thousand in number, so why must we do what was done before by billions of people who almost destroyed the planet?"

Anuhea, contradicting her husband, Kaikoa, said, "Because our young people are leaving preferring to live in Port Villa, and even other places. Places as far away as Fiji and New Caledonia. Not only do we need to grow our population, but we need to keep them here on Aneityum. Mea is right, without further development of our scarce resources we will become obsolete and void of citizens. I say we all work on developing. . . what did you call it, the internet? And also global communication capability just as Mea proposes."

"And new fuel sources are necessary for our electricity and transportation. Also, our music and other art. When we run out of these supplies in Port Villa then we will be back to our old and less enjoyable place," Ruru offered in support.

It was quiet in the new community building with the exception of the rain on the thatched roof. After listening to the pleas of the ministers Osh spoke again. "Ruru, do our people still enjoy dancing and singing—as we have for centuries— more or the same with your new music devices?"

"I would say more . . . oh wait, maybe the same. We now have guitars, drums and new apparatus for our dancing and singing for almost fifteen years, but the joy is still the same. However, today we have more people making the music and I think less dancing." Ruru paused before continuing. "I don't know Osh, if you are asking me if our new instruments makes our lives more joyful I don't think so. But if it makes us more involved in the music, then the answer is yes. But, I must admit, that if we were to lose all our new instruments then we would still dance and sing as we did before in a very joyful way."

"Mea, what about food and shelter? Has there been any new foods that we have eaten that has made our stomachs more full?" Not waiting for her to answer, Osh went on. "Or are there any new houses that have provided us with better shelter?" Again not waiting for her response he said, "So, I am asking all of you, are we a happier community now than we were before, even with all the worlds wealth? Or has all these newfound possessions hurt our souls and made problems we have never had to worry about before?"

At first no one said anything weighing Osh's questions very carefully. Even though he had directed them to Mea all the elders felt that Osh was also asking them to join in on the debate. An elder woman named Satina, in a gentle, but strong voice took up the gauntlet and answered Osh's questions.

"Mea is right," Satina, who was around eighty years old started her rebuttal. "And Osh is right, but the two are not mutually exclusive. There is no reason that we shouldn't learn more and do more to make our world a more interesting place, but not at the expense of our happiness and joy. But, thinking about what has happened on the planet I propose that Mea pursue this internet thing she talks about so that we may communicate with whoever else is still out there."

Silently waiting for her comment to soak in the concept of other humans in the world had never been voiced at council meetings before. Satina continued, "It is unlikely that our small group of people here in Waitara is the only place left on the whole earth where humans still live. But those of us who want to stay here and live as we have for centuries should not be compelled to adopt new things if they make them uncomfortable." Her public revelation that other life may still be out there put an added responsibility to Mea's argument that everyone needed to consider.

It was ironic that Kaikoa had said to Anuhea, "I think that maybe our people were chosen by our ancestors to find any others still out there and make the world over again," just moments before the meeting started. The two justice ministers smiled at each other after Satina proclaimed the same.

And so it was adopted by council that Mea and her scientists and engineers continue to pursue how to re-establish the internet and gain all the knowledge in the world that it promised to offer. Meanwhile, they would carefully conserve their store of fuel so that electrical, and transportation needs would still be met, but a major mission for their community would now be to find other humans on earth who may still be alive. If Mea's internet quest would serve that end, then all the more reason to pursue it.

* * *

Weeks later, on a day in March, after they had a communal dinner and were home in their own house, Anuhea told Kaikoa something that shocked him. "You say that Mea has been working on this plan for almost six months and you now are just telling me about it? Didn't you think it was important that I know that you and, what is it, twenty or more citizens would be going on this journey?" Kaikoa asked her.

"I didn't know that I would be going until Mea asked if it wouldn't be wise for us to make this voyage. If we do find others alive then at least one of us would be needed to guide their actions. What if they turn out hostile, or indifferent to our plight?" Anuhea explained to her husband.

"And you think it's wise that Malosi accompany you on this dangerous journey?" Kaikoa was speaking about their fifteen-year-old son who was always interested in sea travel and was taught to navigate by the sun and stars from his grandfather Osh.

"Malosi is an educated man now who has been studying the ship for almost a half a year." Anuhea explained the circumstances surrounding their son's involvement in the venture. "They found this luxury yacht anchored in Vila Bay and he fell in love with it instantly. It was named The Atomic and was built around thirty years ago. The ship's log showed that it had arrived in Port Vila in November of 2033, trying to escape death from the great plague. It sailed from California in America, stopping once to refuel in Hawaii. But death and abandonment was already widespread there, so they continued on to Port Vila, but within two weeks of their arrival they too succumbed."

"Why has Malosi never told me about his discovery and that he could sail such a complex thing as a . . . what did you call it? A luxury yacht?" Kaikoa, who spent most of his time reading social science and poetry or political science literature, was not interested in hard science topics. But knowing his son's love of the sea, taught to him by his grandfather Osh, it didn't surprise him that he would want to go on this planned sea journey of over 3,500 nautical miles to Australia.

Anuhea filled him in on the plan. "There would be twenty people going, at least fifteen would be scientists and engineers who were also experienced sailors. I and two others would be from our government and two elders would also be asked to go. But that may change as we get closer to leaving. Malosi would stay in my cabin with me and as the youngest member of the crew he would have to listen to what I told him to do."

"Like that will happen," Kaikoa said smiling at his son's well-known adventurous and independent behavior.

"He will also be the lead navigator on the boat. Even though they have a very advanced navigation system on board many of the satellites that are used by the system are getting old and unreliable. So, Malosi's navigation skills might be needed for that purpose as well," Anuhea said.

She also explained that they would all be dressed in western style clothes and have western style haircuts so as not to scare any white people that may be alive in Australia. In addition they had all been studying English and talking to each other in English even though they had only heard spoken English and western music on very old tape recorders using even older batteries still found in stores on the islands of Vanuatu.

After quietly absorbing Anuhea's plan Kaikoa told her, "You know we will miss you, but I think it wise that only one of us travel so far from home. I guess, I mean two of us if Malosi is asked to go as you suggest. And when will you leave?" Kaikoa was noticeably sad when he asked his wife about Mea's planned trip to Australia.

"In mid-May, if the elders approve of our venture by next month."

* * *

When the elders announced the trip to the rest of the community showing them pictures of the ship and all its features lots of people wanted to go on Mea's expedition to rebuild the internet. Most didn't fully understand why she chose Australia and why they wanted to get an atomic submarine as a power source to run their electrical network, but they accepted what Mea told them They wished a safe journey for the twenty people chosen by Mea and her staff, and they all offered any help they could to guarantee its success.

Ruru planned a celebratory feast with music and dance when they left so that they would have good memories of Waitara on their voyage. There were lots of tears and smiles as the community watched them leave on their small boat trip up to Port Vila. There they would board the ironically named yacht Atomic on Friday, May 19, 2051, for Australia.

The crew was more than anxious to get underway for the six-day cruise to Port Melbourne for refueling, then another six days to the Royal Australian Navy base (RAN) Stirling, situated on the west coast of Australia. The base, located on Garden Island, was near the city of Perth.

After arriving in Melbourne on May 25, and after refueling the Atomic, they found an intact tour bus at the port, fully fueled and still capable of traveling. So they drove it into the city.

The apartments, office buildings, restaurants and shops, roads, cars, houses bridges, railroads, and on and on, all of which the team had seen in pictures before leaving Vanuatu, left them no less awe struck when seeing them for real. They felt a strong need for the previous residents to take them around, show them their city and explain all the things that made it run. And it left them incredibly sad that no humans other than them were anywhere to be found.

Six days later when they reached the submarine base on Garden Island they spotted the two monstrous Columbia Class nuclear subs tied up, side-by-side, at one of the piers.

Back in 2021 the United States and Australia struck up a deal to build the ultra-expensive (over ten billion dollars for each) as deterrents to China's ever-expanding takeover of the Pacific Ocean. By the early 2030s two boats had been completed and finished sea trials and were permanently stationed at RAN Stirling. When the plague came about three years later the ships were decommissioned and put out of service, but still maintained their full potential if someone just came in who knew how to start them up; Malosi and Mea were two such people who knew how.

It was Mea's plan to operationalize one of the boats and tow it back to Vanuatu where it would serve as the country's electrical power source, and where she planned to restart the internet. The subs each had two reactors which could generate around two hundred megawatts of electrical output. That would be more than enough power to supply Vanuatu whose population today still hovered at a thousand souls living for the most part in Waitara, Aneghowhat and Port Villa.

Mea had carefully laid out her plan selecting Australia's atomic sub as her source for power. She knew it was nearby, could easily, in a relative sense, be connected to a grid and would not require fuel for another thirty or more years. It was a well thought out engineering solution and she had trained many young people to put it all together.

But her star was Malosi. Even at his youthful age he showed a unique talent for engineering and seamanship that set him apart from his peers. She groomed him for this task and the two of them were the first humans to board the sub in almost twenty years. The rest of the crew remained outside on the pier waiting to see what happened after Mea and Malosi went inside. For over an hour they heard nothing.

When the two came out with smiles on their faces Mea said to her anxious team members, "Well, are you all ready for a tour of our new electric power plant?"

Uproarious cheers went out from the crew as they all ran to the hatch for their chance to see this marvelous piece of technology that was now their country's own.

* * *

Starting the power plant of a nuclear vessel is not just a simple matter of pushing a button. First they had to be sure that the twenty-year-old auxiliary batteries still had enough power to turn on the emergency lights and initiate the nuclear engines power up procedure. Mea was thrilled beyond belief when the batteries still showed plenty of life to do its tasks. The nuclear plant was already well into the process of powering up when they came top side to notify the rest of her crew.

It would take a few hours after steam could be brought up to full pressure to drive the generator that charged the powerful batteries used to run the sub's drivetrain. Until then they wandered throughout the huge, over five hundred foot long, behemoth totally in amazement at all the fittings, equipment, and supplies still in topnotch working order.

They had an interesting meal, at least for them, prepared from twenty-year-old dried dinner rations that were still edible when they were rehydrated and cooked. But nothing surprised them more than what awaited them when they came out in the evening after having dinner in the mess hall.

As they walked out of the sub's hatch they saw them there—about a dozen—sitting or squatting on the pier. They straightaway recognized them as Australian Aboriginal People with their dark skin, wild hair, and painted bodies. Even though several carried spears no hostility was demonstrated, just curiosity.

"Well, no need for the internet now," Mea said as she looked in wonderment at the entourage.

Her group just stopped and stared before Anuhea began to speak to them in a calm voice and with a broad smile waving her arms to show no weapons and saying in her native Bislama language, "Thank you for meeting with us," and repeating it over and over. She slowly, but purposefully walked over to the gangplank to meet the visitors while repeating, "Welcome, welcome, . . ." nodding her head. She approached the first visitor and grasped his hand saying, this time in French, "Bienvenu, welcome," and in Bislama, "Welkam, Halo."

The gentleman smiled and said in his native Port Jackson Pidgin English, "How you dey? Mi Jabiru," Anuhea recognized it instantly as to mean, 'how are you today? My name is Jabiru.' When the two quite different Indigenous Peoples met and discovered that they could communicate with each other cheers and laughter broke out as they all rushed to hug each other and discover how each survived the great plague.

It was a time for celebration knowing that the world was not empty of all other people. Mea's team was thrilled that Satina's proclamation earlier in the year, that it was, '*Unlikely . . . Waitara is the only place left on the whole earth where humans still live,*' was true.

* * *

Even though the Australian Aboriginal Peoples were literate they had not advanced to the level of science and engineering that the Vanuatu people had. The Australian natives had lived with the Europeans, intermarried, and suffered a host of injustices at the hands of the whites, but still they remained a deeply spiritual and complex people. They kept their culture intact and a number of them stayed in nomadic groups, refusing to settle in one place and avoided mixing with the European settlers. The ones that met with Mea and her group were just one such group of nomads.

Communication, at first, was a bit clumsy, but with both groups speaking in English things became clearer. Though there were many differences between Anuhea and Jabiru, the Australian she first spoke to, there were significant commonalities as well. They danced and sang like the people in Vanuatu and had similar rites and festivals.

But there was something much deeper. Unknown to either of them, both of their ancestors came to their countries at about the same time, somewhere between ten and sixty thousand years ago from Africa through Asia. The amazing thing was that so many cultural habits from so many years ago were still imbedded in their DNA, and it was that relationship that joined them together. But there was another ancient tie that bonded them even tighter and that came out in one of their meetings.

"So, it was you who was watching me," Malosi told Jabiru. "I could not see you, but I knew you were there. Why didn't you make yourselves known to us before?"

"I had to be sure you weren't carrying the disease that took everyone else from our place," he answered, "But when we saw you entering the great boat we knew we had to approach you."

"How come you never told me that you were being watched?" Anuhea asked her son.

"Because it was just a feeling that eyes were on me, but nothing else. They were so well concealed that I wasn't sure if I wasn't just imagining it," he told her.

"Your son is very interesting to us," Jabiru said in a very serious way, "Look at this picture; do you recognize him?" he said showing Anuhea a picture from an old National Geographic magazine of the Easter Island *moai*, or the famous large carved stone figures with heads all having the same facial characteristics.

"Well, what do you know, they do look a little like Malosi, I guess. But Malosi has a much nicer face. So why did you find that so interesting?" Anuhea asked.

"Our ancient tradition tells us that these stones are faces of our ancestors who we believe came from another world. Seeing, Malosi, we thought that maybe our ancestors were sending him to us with a message from them. The tradition also tells us that a young man will bring us that message."

"I find that very interesting that you might think my son is a messenger from the beyond, but I can assure you that he is just a boy. An incredibly talented boy, but still just a boy," Anuhea said smiling politely, but none the less slightly worried that her hosts might want to keep Malosi there.

A few days later when all the preparations for towing the sub back to Aneityum were finished, Jabiru appeared but this time with just two other people: his wife and son. They were dressed in western garb and had some baskets packed with their belongings. They approached Mea and, not actually asking for permission, but rather just bluntly stating that they would be going with them to Vanuatu. Mea suggested that they take their request, as she put it, to Anuhea since she represented the government.

Meeting with Anuhea, Jabiru made his claims clearer. "This is not a request. The ship is ours and we are letting you borrow it, so I have been directed by my people to go with you and our submarine to learn how you will use it. We have another one here and one day we may wish to use it the same way."

Anuhea thought about what the man said and realized that he was right. The sub was theirs and by all rights they should have asked permission to borrow it. She agreed that Jabiru and his family would be welcome in Vanuatu and that they could stay as long as they pleased. But there was no promise that she could ever return them back to Australia. With that caveat they agreed and took their belongings aboard the Columbia class vessel and made themselves at home.

Malosi along with a crew of eight took control of the sub while the other seven engineering members of the expedition team staffed the Atomic, which would tow the sub. Malosi's crew was fully capable of running the sub but only on the surface because they had never tried to submerge it. Following the same route home stopping to refuel once again but at an easier port than Melbourne, to maneuver the two vessels, they arrived at Aneityum seven days after the refueling task.

They were happy to be home and Ruru once again prepared a feast and ceremony where the entire population would be introduced to the sub's owner Jabiru and his family and have an opportunity to see the sub up close. It was a happy day on the small island of Aneityum

CHAPTER TEN

As time passed and the sub was permanently installed in Port Vila, a couple hundred of the younger members of the Waitara community moved to the now electrified city where the Parliament House was turned into a university, the Waitara Institute of Higher Education. The sub's nuclear plant was large, but not large enough to run the entire system with all the lights, refrigerators, heating, and cooling systems of a city that size, so they turned off large sections of the grid. But they kept the computers on at the parliament house for the engineering and science students, who were most of the enrollees.

Jabiru's son, Djalu, was educated at the institute and specially tutored by Malosi on how to run the sub. In 2055, Jabiru and his family were taken back to Australia on the Yacht that brought them to Vanuatu in 2051. Back in Australia, Jabiru's son would teach other members of their community how to utilize the remaining sub. Jabiru permanently gifted Waitara the sub that they borrowed as payment for training them; Jabiru promised to contact them once they had trained their people to operate global communication equipment.

A few years earlier the international airport in Port Vila had been opened and a flight school was put in place for the adventurous ones wanting to fly. By 2058 they already had flown to other countries; New Caledonia, Fiji, and Hervey Bay, in Australia, and other places in the south pacific where modern travel was in existence. They started out with single engine jet aircraft that could cover 2,000 nautical miles, at a speed of around five hundred miles an hour, but as they went to larger and larger airports they came upon larger planes capable of ranges of almost 10,000 nautical miles. But the infrastructure needed to maintain and service those larger planes was not there.

In 2058 Mea was still the director of the institute, and Malosi at just 22 years old was one of her leading professors. In the seven years since the importation of nuclear power the overwhelmingly vast transportation and communications infrastructure left in the rest of the world was still mostly idle. Mea had hopes that some of it would be restored by her students. The internet was what she hoped for, and she was able to see bits and pieces of it on some of her computers where cloud storage and communication satellites were still operating under thirty-year-old nuclear and solar powered systems.

Then one hot and rainy day in February, the communication center at the Waitara Institute was startled to receive a communication from Garden Island, Australia; "Halo from Jabiru. Are you there?" And the first transnational radio gram in the new world was delivered.

Mea was pleased beyond words. Her dream, though far from fully realized, was beginning to take shape and she strongly believed that with advanced airplane pilot and maintenance training, travel to the rest of the world, like it once was, was inevitable.

Making contact with Jabiru was the opening of a new international venture, whereby the two groups of people with a combined population of less than five thousand souls would rediscover the world. At the small airport on Garden island a school was started jointly run by Jabiru's son and one of Malosi's senior students to learn airplane maintenance and flying large aircraft. Within two short years they were flying jets out of Melbourne's airport.

* * *

"So, my dear intelligent friend," Jabiru was saying to Anuhea on a visit back to Vanuatu on his son's business jet, a sleek Embraer Phenom 300, "what is next for our two countries?"

They were meeting in a nicely kept guest house on a serene beach in Anegowhat that was used for a variety of local governmental functions. A couple of hundred Waitara citizens had moved to the larger village to work the farms and live in a place with electricity and other amenities like plumbing. Most didn't want to move to Port Villa because it seemed so desolate.

"How about music and storytelling? Those tales you told me of those many years ago are still fresh in my mind. I think we need to share our cultures more because I think we have more in common than differences. I also think we need to establish new standards, like dates and language so it will be easier to talk with each other," Anuhea offered as starters.

"And to all others we may meet in the years to come," Jabiru replied.

"Hmm . . . I think that that may be more difficult than is possible for just our two countries of so few people. Unless the *others* live in an area of around a few thousand-kilometer radius, or our populations explode beyond all imaginable limits, it will not happen in ours, or our children's lifetime," she said. Pausing a bit she continued, "But tell me again what you know about the great plague?"

Jabiru explained how he remembered how it all happened. He was around fifty years old when the earlier illness, a brain death they called DEF, was destined to kill everyone, so he and his group of nomads stayed away from the European population. Jabiru went on to tell Anuhea, "Then a couple of years, or so, later a cure was found but it required that the entire world be treated. Having recalled the pandemic of 2020 and how a vaccine prevented the dreaded Covid disease, people were more than happy to be treated. But soon after most humans were cured of the brain death, a new disease, an incurable cancer, was visited on the earth and all who were treated for the DEF began to die."

"Did everyone die, there must have been some who, like us, were not treated?" Anuhea said.

Jabiru explained, "A lot of the European people, were not treated, but then they eventually died of the DEF. But my people survived like your people, and I'm certain that others in the world, like ours, who were not susceptible to DEF, nor did they received the treatment, also survive. They must be all around the world and it is our duty to find them and join with them as I believe our ancestors would have wanted us to do."

Jabiru, pausing for emphasis added, "You have no belief in a greater being like the Europeans do, other than your ancestors guidance, which we have too. I believe that some people, people who resemble your son Malosi and his grandfather Osh visited the world from somewhere else. That was way, way in the past, long before the world was like it is today. It was those people who gave us something the other animals did not have, and we were chosen to grow and take care of our world for a reason that I do not yet know." Looking a bit troubled but with conviction he continued. "We must find the others who are like us and continue to do what our ancestors wanted us to do. This I believe and so must you or else you would not be doing what you're doing."

"And what is it, Jabiru, that we are doing?

"Having Mea and Malosi Teach us the way of nature and how to use its secrets to do marvelous things. And taking my son, Djalu, and teaching him all he now knows about science and engineering. You, my revered friend, have given us the power to reach our reason for living," Jabiru told her.

"Oh, Jabiru, I think you give me and my people too much credit for what is happening now. I fear that most of my people would simply rather think about eating and making babies and not be bothered with learning about the complexities of nature. I also think that that may be true of your people as well. I would also like to believe that all we are doing has some greater purpose, but when I think of the enormous task ahead with such a limited capacity to do it I do get discouraged."

"If you are telling me that we may not reach the others in our time here, well I do believe you. But that doesn't mean that our children, or our children's children, or even more generations can't do it in the future. So it is up to us to make certain that could happen," the almost eighty-year-old Jabiru declared. "But you forgot to add music and dancing as two other activities that our people think about all the time," he said with a broad smile.

"Yes, and they both lead to more eating and baby making," Anuhea said, also smiling broadly.

* * *

By the year 2062 CE the two countries agreed to calling the year 2034 the year 1 Nouveau Calendrier, French for New Calendar. The year was re-constituted into twelve months of thirty days with a five-day holiday period at the end of December for celebrating their summer and looking forward to another year of prosperity and learning and exploring.

But once every four years the holiday would be extended to six days with the extra day used only for a celebration of eating, dancing, and singing, and yes, making babies. The year, 4 NC, was the first leap year and 2062, or 28 NC was the seventh leap year in the new calendar. Each of the holidays was named after an elder, either a dead one or a living one, but this year's sixth day, or *Six de Vacance*, was named after Jabiru who had died two months earlier.

There was still considerable mourning being felt in the two countries. A Zoom like meeting of the festivities were viewed by most citizens of the then known world, and the shared grieving and shared celebration did much to temper the sadness felt by all.

"We will miss the wise council of Jabiru, and we will continue to pursue his dream of finding the others in the world that are still alive and of whom we may, or may not share common ancestors," Anuhea told the viewers.

"And we will dedicate ourselves to his principles of peace, tolerance, patience and understanding of all the people and creatures that share the Earth," Kaikoa added.

"And his joy of life," his son, Djalu, further noted.

"But most important, we will commit ourselves to the preservation of our planet's delicate balance between life and death and never allow it to reach the precipice of self-destruction that occurred in the old calendar time," Mea said finishing the invocation.

"So, let us celebrate with our traditional dancing and singing and joy that we have reserved for this once in a four-year day," Kaikoa said to start the festivities off.

And so with a separation of a few thousand miles the two countries acted as one, and in spite of the rain, humidity and heat they danced like they had for centuries before . . . only now the musical accompaniment sounded better.

* * *

Unknown to the Vanuatuan and Australian first nations peoples, in a secluded part of China around thirty miles from the large city of Guiyang, there existed an isolated mountain village called Taiyan. The village was populated by a few thousand Hmong citizens, or Miao people as they preferred to be called, and the agrarian lifestyle there went on pretty much as it had for thousands of years.

The village residents, although they were relatively isolated, were literate and had some modern amenities, like a water and sanitation system and access to books and literature. But that was about it. The residents were well aware of the world around them, and although they avoided the DEF pandemic, and the treatment designed to cure it, the loss of the 4.5 million citizens of Guiyang was still mourned by them.

Kub Yang, the village shaman, and his wife Che had been dealing with the loss of life from Guiyang and a few nearby villages for nearly thirty years. That was true even though nobody from their village had died from DEF or its subsequent cure. Their village preferred to remain isolated, and they did not want to find out what happened in Guiyang. But a few years earlier, in 2060, at the bidding of some of his younger citizens, Kub had agreed to let a team investigate the large modern city of Guiyang to see what they could learn from its demise, but most important to see if it was safe to go there.

The exploration party was divided into five two person teams, each team was assigned to search and report back on the condition of a different part of the city. Once in the city the investigation teams soon adjusted to its size and grandeur and were fascinated by all the amenities, like gas and electricity, that the city offered its residents.

Reporting back from their excursion the young leader of the ten-member expedition party testified, "There were many fires that we think were started by animals setting off gas fires from appliances. It was hard to tell when they occurred or if any members of the city died from them. But most of the city remained untouched. Vehicles still looked capable of running, but we did not try to run any."

"So, what is that you want to do? Are you certain that the plague is gone and that you are not carrying it?" Kub asked them.

"We would like to go back and stay longer. There is so much to learn from the place, and we would like to take more people with us. Since going there none of us have been sick or even feeling different, so we feel that it's safe."

"We also believe that there are more people in the world who are like us; alive and wondering how to join up with others," a young woman, named Chi, from the team threw out, much to Che's surprise since Chi was her daughter.

"And why should we try to make ourselves known to them? Visitors to our community have always meant trouble for our people. I would hope, Kub, that you won't allow them to contact others," Che pleaded.

"It's not my decision," Kub said. "It's up to all the village officers. I will tell them what you have requested, and they will let you know," he said.

With that it was decided that the young team of explorers request to further explore the city, and to try and contact whoever else might be out there would be given to the village chief. It would be up to him and his councilors to decide, but Che's objection to contact others would also be noted.

* * *

The village council agreed to let a group of around fifty explore Guiyang further, learn what they could about the great plague and how to use the modern equipment, but they were told specifically not to try and contact the rest of the world. Naturally, they didn't listen to the council's directive.

On an early January day in the year 2062, or 28 NC, the Guiyang expedition led by Kub, and Che's thirty-five-year-old daughter Chi excitedly informed the council that they had heard from other parts of the world.

"You were specifically told not to contact the others, why did you do that?" Kub asked her.

"Oh father, you gave us an impossible order if we were to explore the modern devices. In any case, our satellite communication equipment had picked up signals from a place in the south Pacific called Port Vila, in the country of Vanuatu. We haven't answered them yet . . ."

"So you haven't contacted them," Kub said.

"Not yet, but we thought it best that we let the council know that it is our intent to do so. Their communications are in three languages that we have figured out: English, French and Bislama. Bislama is an English based dialect our language experts tell us. We can communicate in English so we decided that with council approval we would let them know we are here. Port Vila is over eight thousand kilometers away from us, so it is not likely they would be able to come here."

After much deliberation and still with Che's objection the council agreed to let the team contact the citizens of Port Vila, but not to invite them to China. They agreed to a cultural exchange of information and understanding, but most important, they would be asked if they knew how safe the rest of the world was.

A document six pages long describing their conditions in China and who the Hmong people were was prepared and sent by the same international communications satellite from Guiyang to Port Vila. And with that transmission the new world's population had grown significantly larger, almost doubling. Chi and her team, now housed in one of Guiyang's modern, but smaller, hotels waited anxiously for a response.

The message from the Hmong team was sent out in the morning, when it was three hours later, or early afternoon, in Port Vila. The response was almost immediate.

"Halo! We have been expecting you for some time now, and we are so happy to know that there is more life in the world. We haven't read your entire message yet, but that doesn't matter. What matters is that you are there. As soon as our authorities digest what you've sent we will respond with the hope of setting up a continued dialogue for peace, growth and understanding. For now we remain your family in love and friendship. My name is Anuhea, and along with my husband, Kaikoa, we are the joint directors of the Ministry of Justice. I cannot wait to continue to know you better."

* * *

With three different nationalities in the world now connected by communication, and probably soon by air travel, the world rejoiced. Even Che was moved by the response and anxious to find out who these people of the south were and what they had to offer them.

It seemed only fitting that the three community's origins were from Indigenous Peoples, and that these wonderful subjects would once again start to populate the Earth. But this time with full knowledge of the earth's vulnerability to unbounded growth and irresponsible human behavior. Maybe this time around it would end up differently and principles of sharing, loving, and the firm belief that all species can live together in harmony would rule the planet.

Only time will tell . . . only time.